LOVE *at* DEEP DUSK

A PENNSYLVANIA STORY

by

J. HARVIE WILKINSON III

MILFORD
HOUSE

an imprint of Sunbury Press, Inc.
Mechanicsburg, PA USA

MILFORD HOUSE

an imprint of Sunbury Press, Inc.
Mechanicsburg, PA USA

For information about special discounts for bulk purchases, please contact Sunbury Press Orders Dept. at (855) 338-8359 or orders@sunburypress.com.

To request one of our authors for speaking engagements or book signings, please contact Sunbury Press Publicity Dept. at publicity@sunburypress.com.

FIRST MILFORD HOUSE PRESS EDITION: February 2022

Set in Adobe Garamond Pro | Interior design by Crystal Devine | Cover by Ashley Shumaker | Edited by Jennifer Cappello.

Publisher's Cataloging-in-Publication Data
Names: Wilkinson, J. Harvie, author.
Title: Love at deep dusk : a Pennsylvania story / J. Harvie Wilkinson.
Description: First trade paperback edition. | Mechanicsburg, PA : Milford House Press, 2022.
Summary: What would you do if the person you loved most betrayed you in the most horrible fashion? Is forgiveness the solution, or would it only amplify the pain? In *Love at Deep Dusk: A Pennsylvania Story*, Leah must confront these questions. In struggling for answers, the novel will take you on a journey through the Keystone State, from the skyscrapers of Philadelphia to Central Pennsylvania's apple country.
Identifiers: ISBN : 978-1-62006-576-1 (softcover).
Subjects: FICTION / Romance / Contemporary | FICTION / Romance / Clean & Wholesome | FICTION / Small Town & Rural | FICTION / Family Life / General | FICTION / Family Life / Marriage & Divorce | FICTION / Legal.

Product of the United States of America
0 1 1 2 3 5 8 13 21 34 55

Continue the Enlightenment!

To the teachers who instilled in me
a love of literature.

PROLOGUE

One early fall evening, as the three Richards children were playing tag and hide-and-seek, an only child named John came down the street and asked to join them. No one knew much about his parents, who kept largely to themselves.

Their games could use a fourth, so Leah was quick to say, "Come on!" John was glad to jump in. From that moment on, he became part of Richards family life in far more than games.

1

Was Gloria smiling? Or smirking?

Her skirt as always was two inches too high. And she was always standing a foot too close to John.

"How are you, Leah?"

"Fine." (Until you came.)

"Will we see you at Pizza Hut Saturday?"

"Not sure." (Not if you'll be there.)

John jingled some coins in his pocket. "I guess I should be off now."

Gloria kept smirking. Her expression was no longer a question.

///

"Just what are John's prospects?" her mother had said.

"What?"

"You'll want to marry a man with prospects, Leah, that's what."

"Who's talking marriage, Mom? I'm seventeen!"

"I see the way you look at him, Leah. Money helps love along, dear girl. Love can't go it alone."

"Don't you think a man can be more than what's in his wallet?" Leah felt compelled to ask several days later.

"I don't think, Leah, I just do. Thinking's a waste of time. Here, take these keys. Your father's car's in the shop. You like to drive. Go pick him up."

Margaret Richards had grown up poor. Her parents died before she was twelve, and life left the teenage girl to scavenge, grasping for help wherever she could find it. Work had beaten the softness from her hands, but not their defiant energy.

"One day, Leah, you will be hard up against it."

"I hope not," Leah said.

"I hope not, too," her mother said.

///

So, the daughter was cast alone upon her thoughts. Quite immediate thoughts, in fact.

It seemed impossible to steal a pure moment with John. If her stellar grades dipped ever so slightly, the car keys were confiscated. She could not afford that now. The Woodson Whirl, the school's big dance, was not far off.

The Whirl was pure Woodson, shielding the small town from every outside gaze. Who went with whom was of supreme importance, precisely because it mattered not in Philadelphia or to the rest of the world.

Would John ask her? She had to know.

John, on his end, did not know himself.

"Do you think you'll take Leah?" his friend Henry asked.

"Do you think she's cute?"

"Sort of," said Henry. "But so is Gloria."

It was true, John thought. He had options. Leah was such interesting company, and their friendship went way back. But Gloria was oh-so blonde, a beauty, a catch. Especially for a non-athlete. For a good but not great student. For an average guy.

///

As Whirl Night arrived, Leah found herself entertaining uncharitable thoughts, like how long had it been since a light flicked on in Gloria's brain. She'd heard that John and Gloria were attending the Whirl together thanks to the local rumor mill, which raced through town faster than fire through a hayfield. Didn't even have the decency to tell me himself, she thought as she turned for understanding to her mirror where a keen gaze awaited her, though one that stopped short of being severe. People always called her precise features "interesting," but she worried that John hadn't found them so. The mirror didn't catch her suitably trim figure, but Leah knew it to be. Oh well, the fact that John and Gloria were going didn't mean three words would pass between them. Why should she even care what John thought of her? John be damned!

Leah flopped onto her bed and read—or tried to. She had turned down all three guys who'd asked her, not because they weren't nice enough, but simply because they weren't John. *Ugh!* She snapped her book shut. Why wouldn't the whole subject just leave her alone?

Woodson High School was Woodson's only high school. Most everyone in town had been there or was going there, and those who settled in Woodson as adults became truly acculturated when their children attended—where else—Woodson High. There were many places of worship in Woodson, but there would always be just one high school—everyone, it seemed, would share at least the singular experience of a Woodson High education. At night, it was whispered, the spirits of classes and instructors past emerged to stalk the hallways, so much of Woodson's history had the venerable old building seen.

But by day, the halls were like high school corridors everywhere, cliquish and rude, designed to absorb endless rounds of personal and physical abuse. No normal hallway would tolerate what high school corridors did. No normal, healthy feeling could ever flourish there. Student lockers were the surest gauge of popularity. Their doors seemed to slam shut in purposeful unison, and Leah always checked out John's to see who was gathered round. Gloria was a regular, of course, bestowing her best smiles. Not to worry; Leah would out-compete her in class. A crush might bloom in the hallway, but nothing so real as romance. Or so Leah hoped as she stumbled into Mr. Carson's AP history class. This was her turf; Gloria was no AP and nowhere to be found in any course that challenged the mind.

Mr. Carson was made for bow ties, and many graduated from Woodson having never seen him without one. He had been teaching at Woodson for what seemed like forever, a monument in his own way to the changeless core of ever-changing life. He was connected to history to be sure, especially living only a few miles from Gettysburg, but wholly disconnected from what students might be thinking outside the Civil War. He had grown up in Gettysburg, gone to Gettysburg College, and his one great regret in life was that Meade, and not some more aggressive and famous general, had commanded the prevailing Union forces there.

"John, who was the better Union general, Grant or Sherman?"

"Well, they both seemed good."

"Yes, but who was better?"

A scrawled paper passed suddenly before John's eyes but missed Mr. Carson's notice. "Grant, because he had the tougher opponent."

Mr. Carson seemed mildly surprised and oddly satisfied.

"Leah," John said later that afternoon, "did you think I couldn't answer on my own?"

Silence.

"Do you think I always need your help?"

"Sometimes you do." No sooner had she said it than she wished it back.

"Thanks, but no thanks," he said.

///

Woodson's football stadium was bursting with noise. "Go Red! Go White! Go Woodson! Go! Go! Go!" The cheerleaders yelled. Friday nights in fall were Hero Nights at Woodson, which meant that Leah's brother, Hank, was in uniform. The color, the status, the team spirit conveyed by uniforms took hold of Hank's fancy early. "You really don't have to wear that Number 15 to dinner," his mother admonished him.

The eyes of Woodson were upon the moment. The guys clapped and shouted as they broke the huddle. The vendors seemed more intent on the game than on selling their dogs. The old-timers imagined that, after thirty years, they were once again making tackles for Woodson High. The game was close. Groups of fans and strangers alike hugged and high-fived after every Woodson score. And why not? Winning meant bragging rights for everyone for miles around. Even church seemed livelier on a winning weekend.

Leah and her little sister, Ellen, shouted with pride from the stands as their running back brother gained another six yards on an end-around.

John and some other guys in the stands had their own little huddle on the twenty, which a group of girls now invaded en masse.

"How 'bout some company," one called.

"Girls? Company?" The guys all laughed.

"Want to join your friends?" John asked at halftime when the other girls had been shooed off or insulted away.

"In a bit," Leah replied, quietly hoping they could walk the sidelines together.

At this point, their talk stopped as the Woodson Song, to the tune of "Aura Lee," washed over the crowd. The alums who'd sung it the longest now sang it the loudest:

> *Woodson High, Woodson High,*
> *To Woodson far and near.*
> *Forever in our hearts we'll hold*
> *Woodson close and dear.*
>
> *The years may come, the years may go*
> *Our youth may pass us by*
> *But always young in memory*
> *Are our days at Woodson High.*

"These songs may seem sappy to all but the singers," John said as the last sounds floated off. "But they love it. It's their song, no one else's."

By the fourth quarter, as the night chill set in, it became clear that the Red and White would win. Hank was having a good game. "What makes him so good?" Leah wondered aloud. "He's kind of small."

"Confidence," John said. "Hank thinks he can do anything."

"Can someone work at confidence? Or does it have to come naturally?"

"I have to work at it," John replied.

Leah took his hand. "That's not all bad," she said.

"Maybe," he replied, adjusting his fingers twined with hers but not pulling away. "But when I walk into a gathering, I have to shore myself up. Hank walks into a room like he owns the world."

///

Homework time in the Richards household was more often than not a communal enterprise. The family's home had become something of a meeting place, and the whole thing was driving Margaret Richards to distraction. The children's friends tromped through, even on week-nights, and often without books in hand, leaving her carefully tended house and yard a place to "waste time." Some of the visitors might set out to court her son or daughters, perhaps even snare one in eventual matrimony—a thought that kept Margaret Richards continually on guard. Those she couldn't chase off she sought to regulate; a set of dis-regarded rules adorned the entrance to the home. That she was losing her lonely struggle against backsliding civilization made her all the more determined to soldier on.

And she was indeed a force, neither to be ignored nor trifled with, an unforgettable lesson the unsuspecting had to learn. John was perhaps the most frequent visitor to the household, a position that left him in the crosshairs.

On and on Margaret Richards went one testy evening, insisting the principal at Woodson was too lenient, "students running circles around him," until John came quietly to his defense.

"Who do you think you are?" she glowered. "Family? Is Richards your last name?"

"Mother!" Leah shouted. It was the first time she had dared to cross her formidable parent in such a way. "Please say you're sorry."

Her mother said nothing of the sort and disappeared into the kitchen.

John left the house, Leah running after.

"Please, John, sit down," she pleaded, motioning to two rusting chairs nearby. She knew that until that moment he did indeed see him-self almost like family.

"Mother doesn't really mean what she says."

Persuasion, Leah knew, is never just a matter of words, not on things that matter. She ran her slender fingers ever so slowly down his cheek.

"Please come back, John. You'll always be welcome."

///

John did come back several nights later, this time to help Ellen and her boyfriend with plane geometry. "Try looking at it like a puzzle," he said. "You'll have more fun that way."

"Do you always need to study with your boyfriend?" Leah inquired. Ellen made Bs in the courses where Leah had made As—a fact, among others, that made Ellen feel ordinary.

Seeing Ellen turn red, John quickly began discussing the properties of trapezoids. He had a certain gift for explaining things, and more patience than she had, Leah thought.

In fact, Leah was impatient for this little homework session to be over.

"Katie's always running her mouth in class," Leah said when finally alone on the porch with John. The porch was theirs; a contemplative place. Let the action in the Richards household take place inside.

"Don't let it get to you, Leah. Katie's always going to be Katie. Ellen's always going to be Ellen. And no one could be half as bad as this bully in math class who's always pointing to people's pimples and fat and trying to make everyone around him as miserable as he is."

"And you can't stop him?" Leah asked.

"No more than you can stop Katie or turn Ellen into you. People don't much change."

Improving others? Accepting them? Truth on this subject as on so many lay somewhere in between them. Some gray, elusive substance of which each of them possessed but half.

"Let's take a walk," John said, bringing Leah back to Earth.

They left the house at John's leisurely pace. "Leah," he said, "I like walking with you on a sidewalk or in the woods. In fact, I can't imagine a place where I wouldn't enjoy our walks."

"Is that a compliment?" she laughed. "I kind of like the woods."

"Don't get bawdy on me," he chuckled.

"Why not? We're teenagers, aren't we?"

"Right!" he exclaimed, as he drew her against him. "Which means this kiss will never end."

And on their walk, the unspoken thought passed between them that Woodson High would not last forever, not that they even wanted it to. But what would the passage of this sheltered but curiously vulnerable existence mean?

///

Leah glanced out her bedroom window and saw John sauntering up the front walk. She stifled a giggle as she anticipated his knock.

"Hi, John," she said, almost before the door swung open.

"Hey," John muttered.

The two hadn't seen each other since that kiss the other night. He looked down and rubbed the back of his head amid the awkward silence.

Leah started, "Did . . . you come here to see—"

"I came here—sorry," John sighed and started again. "I came here to see if you wanted to take a stroll with me. I left my math assignment in class." He smiled mischievously. "Want to break into the school with me to get it?"

Leah laughed and called over her shoulder, "Going for a walk with John, Mom! Be back soon!" She slammed the door behind her as her mother called something that got lost in the shuffle of the Richards household evening chaos.

Almost at the school, they noticed a dim light on the second floor.

"Wonder if there's thieves up there? Or maybe Mr. Carson rallying the Yanks to victory over the intercom? Or maybe it's just Dracula? I understand the blood tastes better at night."

"Honestly, John, you can spin a story out of anything. Probably just the cleaning crew."

"On a Saturday evening? Not a chance."

"All right, maybe someone just forgot to turn out the light. Happens, you know."

Once inside, through the side door, they spoke only in whispers, grabbing onto one another to navigate the darkened hallways without falling, laughing as they stopped and stumbled. Suddenly, their half-frightened embrace became a full-fledged kiss. Giddy, they fumbled their way toward the illuminated math classroom ahead.

John brushed his fingertips on the sides of Leah's neck. "Want to catch a ghost?" he whispered.

She shushed him, stood resolute, and marched forward in a show of mock bravery. John jogged to catch up to her, but the pair froze in the doorway of the classroom.

The math teacher, Mr. Vaughn, and their classmate, Beth, were hastily gathering themselves. Beth quickly retrieved her skirt from the floor as Mr. Vaughn stammered something about an assignment. Beth furiously buttoned her blouse; Mr. Vaughn began scrawling incoherent equations on the blackboard. One and all sped into action. Beth sprinted down the shadowy hall with her black crossbody bag; John and Leah headed home in a blur. Mr. Vaughn scrambled to his car, not even slowing to release his brake as he exited the parking lot.

"We must report this tomorrow morning," Leah declared as they got over the shock.

She sensed John was hesitant. "Honestly, John, do you always have to be so freaking tolerant?"

"I'm not tolerant. What would you do? Ruin their lives?"

"They're ruining their own lives. He's at least ten years older than Beth."

"He's also a very good math teacher. Maybe the best Woodson High has ever had."

"Stop making excuses!" she shouted.

But John stood his ground. "I also know Beth's parents. They'll never forgive her for this. They'll ship her to boarding school. The age difference won't mean a thing to them."

"How many students is he doing this with? Have you thought about that, John?" her voice still rising.

"There's no others here. Beth is not in his class, Leah. And the two of them have had eyes for each other for some time."

Leah huffed. "John, I'm through discussing this with you. Tomorrow morning I'm in the principal's office with or without you."

"Without me, Leah. And not just for tomorrow morning."

Only then did Leah pause.

"Perhaps, Leah, you could tell Beth that we'll keep this thing quiet if she breaks it off immediately. Paint the full picture of deep trouble. As only you can do."

"I hate keeping secrets."

"Every small town has big secrets, Leah. Even Woodson. People go to their graves here and everywhere with mortifying knowledge."

"Okay, I'll speak to Beth. But no longer to you."

"John," she said a week later, "you're never right. But you're some-times half right, which you were with the Beth – Mr. Vaughn thing."

"Sometimes teens solve things better without grown-ups. My parents have unwittingly taught me that many, many times."

///

Not much woke Hank Richards besides his mother shouting at him to get ready for school in the morning. Tonight, however, he woke to the faint smell of smoke.

Leah was already in the hallway, having dashed out of her room, also fully awake at the ominous scent.

Hank nodded. "I smell it, too. I don't think it's coming from in here. Let's go outside and check."

"Shouldn't we wake Mom and Dad?" Leah whispered urgently.

Hank shook his head. "Not yet. If we find anything, we'll wake them, pronto. Could just be a bonfire or a controlled burn."

Leah hesitated but followed her brother outside.

The Jenkins' house, far and away the most beautiful home on their block, was burning. Leah and her ever-impetuous brother rushed down the street. The blaze consumed the night. Leah chased after Hank, who, in top running back form, was already cutting through the yard of the Jenkins' next-door neighbors.

"What's up?" Hank yelled.

"Step back. We're trying to contain it," the fire chief shouted at Hank as firetrucks, ambulances, and a too-curious clutch of neighbors formed the ghastly scene.

Screams came suddenly from inside.

"Contain it? Baby Jenny's contained *in* it!"

"Stop, Hank!" Leah shrieked as Hank sprinted toward the house.

He was inside—what was left of it—and up the stairs before the firefighters could react. Darting, weaving, dodging flames like would-be tacklers, he reached what he thought would be baby Jenny's room— the only bedroom door still shut. He kicked the door down with more effort than required, the singed hinges loose in the brittle, burned frame. Scooping the hysterical infant and tossing her blanket over both of them, Hank stared around the sweltering, smoky room.

What the flames had spared they now entrapped, sealing off their retreat. "The window. It's stuck! Come on! Come on!" he yelled at the stubborn panes.

"The baby! The baby!" he hollered, as the brute force of burnt arms opened it at last.

Shrieking baby and screaming running back jumped into who-knows-where together, doused in a melee of water and blankets as they hit the safety net.

///

"What are you doing here, Hank?" Coach Ramsey asked the next week. Everyone had heard about the rescue. On seeing Hank approach, his teammates stopped and stared in awe.

"It's practice, Coach." Hank's burns had proved mercifully superficial and treatable, but Coach Ramsey still was not amused.

"I'm sorry, but the trainers say you must miss the Lancaster game."

"You need me, Coach."

"I need you to take a deep breath and be glad you're still alive."

The fire left Hank a hero but Woodson in mourning; thankfulness for the baby's rescue, grief for her family, who had perished in the blaze. Little Jenny's aunt and uncle, who lived outside Philadelphia, had come to collect her next day. She would never again see the person who had saved her life.

///

Woodson, Pennsylvania, was apple country. Its orchards were the envy of producers everywhere, and its canning plants thrived. Apple juice and cider, apple pie and cobbler, apple jam and butter: Leah marveled that the short, somewhat stubby trees could bring forth such a long list of delights. To celebrate this bounty, practically everyone in town made the pilgrimage to the National Apple Harvest Festival, hosted by the nearby town of Biglerville. For the bright young couples of Woodson, the festival was a classic date destination.

But Woodson wasn't just apples. Branch banks, insurance agencies, and brokerage firms gave Main Street the look of a place where life still hummed. Its antique shops drew visitors from around Central Pennsylvania. The shuttered shops of small-town decline had not claimed Woodson, at least not yet, and its civic pride stubbornly resisted despair.

Leah's father was a loan officer and vice president at the largest bank in town and in prime position to accept compliments on Hank's football prowess and (less often) on Leah's academic prizes. He was a far more tolerant person than his wife, meaning that luncheon invitations frequently came his way at work but rather fewer to the couple for dinner.

"Frank, the children must study more," Margaret had warned. She had even handed him the books that she thought the children should master.

But the children were learning something different from their father, namely the rhythms of a small town and how to enjoy a milkshake at Thornton's, even on a weekday afternoon.

Woodson had the advantage of being near Hershey, Pennsylvania—a town named for the great philanthropist and famous chocolatier Milton S. Hershey, and therefore the chocolate capital of the nation. So, the Richards kids were taught the pleasures of sweets early, and later, when it became clear John was a family friend, he was welcomed as a full-fledged member of the chocolate milkshake club.

The big question was who should get the shake with almonds sprinkled on the whipped cream. Once, Mr. Richards awarded it to John as a newcomer. Sometimes Ellen received it as recompense for being the youngest.

"Dad, you're leaving me out," Leah protested at such arbitrary restrictions.

"Leah," he laughed, "I've never known you to allow yourself to be left out of anything."

///

Frank Richards was buried at Woodson Groves on April 4, 1998. Rotarians and vestrymen gathered in grief around their friend. Age 53. Car crash. Small consolation: It was not his fault. Slowly the congregants filed from the graveside, mourning the departed to be sure but newly grateful for their own chance to see another day.

Leah, then a junior, desperately sought comfort, but Ellen was too young, Hank too brash, and her mother too tightly strung and consumed by grief of her own.

"John, you've done your duty," Leah said after he had come by their house three evenings straight.

"It's no duty, Leah. I loved your father. Everyone did."

The spirit of Frank Richards remained a part of Woodson and indeed a part of Leah and John, too. One Thursday afternoon, in the fall of their senior year, John stayed after school for a college admission conference. Leah, who already had been accepted at Harvard, waited for him so they could head home together.

They could have driven, but the sprinkle of fall leaves inspired them to walk, the couple imbibing the simple joy of kicking dry leaves as they made their way.

A repulsive insect landed on the leaves in front of Leah.

"Squash it, John. Quick!"

But he would not.

"How can you be friends with bugs, John?"

"All a part of God's plan, and they're not *bugging* anyone."

"Very funny. I don't know what you plan to do with your life, John, but being a public health inspector is not what I'd recommend."

The day became only more beautiful, and the maple leaves, oddly, inspired Leah to intimacy.

"John, there's something I'd like to ask you."

"That's quite a chilling warm-up," he smiled. "But go ahead."

"Well, you almost never mention your parents, which seems strange. Did they beat you or abuse you in some way?"

"Oh no, nothing like that."

"Well then, what's the deal?"

"It's just that I don't seem to matter to them, one way or the other. Your mom and dad, and you, Hank, and Ellen are all very different, but still, you seemed to matter to each other."

"Are you sure you don't matter? People have different ways of showing love."

"Maybe. I'd just like a touch on the shoulder once in a while. Some connection. We live under the same roof, but I feel like I was dropped there by accident."

She thought before she said, "Can I be the cure for your loneliness?"

"You are, Leah, you are. If, that is, I can offer you something in return."

"Ambition can be a loneliness all its own, I think. So, you're my cure too."

"High school is no place for deep thoughts, even for seniors," he said, putting his arm around her. "Let's go to Thornton's and have a milkshake in memory of a father who cared."

///

Graduations are both joyous and tearful events, made poignant by the feeling that the graduates will all too soon be scattered to the winds. Too often, the graduates suppose their new status confers a license to do as they please, or at least that's what happened to Chip. He drank heavily three weeks before the big day, fell asleep behind the wheel, and never woke up.

Chip and Leah may have been classmates, but they were not especially close. Still, she liked him well enough. He was a threat to none, a pal to all, in Leah's mind "everybody's best friend." Known for his trademark 5th Avenue candy bars, Chip was also a collector—airline stickers, Lincoln pennies, Topps trading cards, you name it. He would be missed.

A memorial service was set. Chip's family went to the same church as the Richards. Leah thought everyone would understand why it was she could not attend.

"But think what your dad would want," John reminded her. "He would want you to be there."

"Please sit beside me then," she said.

/ / /

The big day came ever closer, and the eyes of at least some Woodson High graduates were not seeing far ahead. John and Leah went together to the graduation parties. Gloria became all glamour and waged a pitched battle for John's affections, but it had fallen flat and left her (for the time being) a thing of the past.

Gloria did not go quietly, however. She spread a rumor that Leah had had an abortion until even her erstwhile friends were fed up with the falsehood.

"Stop spreading lies. She's my sister," Ellen had been quick to say.

Leah was headed to Harvard, though not without consternation. She had offered to go to Penn State, where John had been accepted. "A really fine school," she'd argued, "Dad's alma mater," and so on, but the whole topic had exhausted them.

"I can't ask you to do that," he had said.

"Yes, you can. Try me."

"Leah, you're brilliant. A lot smarter than I am. Harvard is for you. I need to be where I'm meant to be. Even if that means being without my best friend."

"That sounds like a put-off. But I get it. I'm crowding you. And by the way, I hate that word you use for me: 'friend.' Sounds like an easy letdown."

And so, to the last bleary hour, she assured him that being young didn't mean one couldn't be lastingly in love, that "High school sweethearts do have happy endings."

"If, in fact, that's what we are," he answered.

She was stunned.

"Leah, I'm sorry. I'm just confused. I can't sort us out."

"Okay," she sighed. "Men need space."

And so, amidst the flurry of hugs and kisses from family, and Leah's marvelous valedictory address, the two graduates left Woodson unresolved.

Hank was off to college where he proved to be a miserable correspondent. Margaret Richards wrote incessantly and checked the mailbox in frustration for letters that never came.

"Hank's busy chasing glory, Mom," Leah would explain. What she did not dare tell her mother was that glory was eluding Hank's grasp.

"I'm sorry, Hank. This is just not going to work."

But why was the running backs coach telling him all this?

"I want to speak with Coach," Hank said.

"What would you like me to tell him for you?"

"Tell him what I lack in size, I make up for in grit. Tell him to give me a chance. Tell him I'll take the last damn seat on the bench, and by senior year I'll score his winning touchdowns."

"Okay, Hank, I'll tell him all that."

"But you're telling me it won't do any good."

Hank was not one to take no for an answer. He donned his pads and appeared on the practice field as if out of nowhere to challenge some of those fancy pants football scholarship recruits to a fifty-yard sprint.

"You're on," one said, and off they went.

Hank, to his shock and dismay, finished near the back of the pack. He was disconsolate. He couldn't bear to tell his friends back home he hadn't made the squad.

It wasn't as though he hadn't been warned. His high school coaches had suggested Division III. But Hank had chosen to walk on at Tennessee. The adoring crowds at the giant Neyland Stadium, the drums, trombones, and tubas, the fabled orange and white, the Vols, the Saturday afternoon adulation . . . to Hank Richards, it sounded great, and he wanted it all.

Even as his dream crashed around him, Hank was not one to be faint-hearted. Intramurals were baby stuff, but there remained a uniform to earn. The military beckoned. He even liked the drills. ROTC was team stuff, the Army would pay his tuition, and at the end of it all would be a position of command.

///

John arrived at Penn State full of anticipation. It was, if not Harvard, a prestigious "public Ivy" whose over 40,000 undergraduates at University Park ensured there would be friends to make and plenty to see and do. JoePa was then in his heyday. "If God isn't a Penn State fan, then why is the sky blue and white," read the bumper sticker. He had never experienced such rowdy and almost vandalistic weekends as when Penn State vanquished its most formidable Big Ten foes. If football wasn't your thing, however, there was Old Main to remind one of the antiquity of learning, and the Life Sciences building to alert you to education's cutting edge.

It was also a place to be aimless if one so desired. The campus acreage was good for walking, the mountains surrounding Happy Valley ideal for longer climbs. The eateries at State College, the nearby town, were full of fun-loving regular guys. Burgers washed down with kegs of beer and talk of sports, cars, girls, and weekend weather. For dessert, ice cream at the Creamery, which had been perfecting its art for almost 150 years. If all that didn't grab you, there were plenty of hiking trips and fishing opportunities nearby. All in all, John thought, a pretty neat place to be.

There was also a sterling education to be had at Penn State, but that was sometimes easier said than done. John was tempted by all kinds of offerings, and it was proving a problem. Options here; choices there; he was awash in indecision. At first, he tried economics and then biochemistry, but graphs and molecular reactions seemed dry to someone of his sensibilities, and while English literature was interesting, he had no idea where it would lead. The same for his charitable work, because

behind. Her attendance at the games eventually dwindled, though she still took the almost obligatory trip to The Game with Yale.

The seminars, of course, were the toughest. It was hard to be the first to offer the most scintillating thought. And when you turned in a paper, it was impossible to escape the thought that your classmates' papers, some of them at least, were going to be very nearly academic perfection.

How to best spend her time came to weigh on Leah's mind. She could try out for the *Crimson* but at the expense of her grades. She needed to do some tutoring, she thought, to round out her résumé, but tutoring was time-consuming and tried her patience. At any rate, she told herself, she had her eye on the ball: Harvard Business or Law was the next step she had to take.

"Can you go to Friday's concert?" If there was any thought that Leah was neglecting her personal life, there was always her blossoming relationship with Bill, a man who was her equal—the thing she never quite knew she wanted until now. A compatible partner for life's ladder, he seemed just right. Without trying, he had made John and Hank seem distant, part of a childhood phase she inexplicably had failed to recognize as such.

She and Bill were both going to be government majors, and already their talks seemed mutually beneficial and full of insight. In a presidential powers class, Bill's paper received an A.

"Congratulations," Leah said over lunch at an old pub named Grendel's Den. There was a surprising edge to her voice.

They'd gradually sensed their relationship was turning competitive. "Maybe we should just not share each other's grades," Bill had offered. Unable to contain their curiosity, however, they continued to compare.

It came down finally to what they call a "pause." A pause, each of them now sensed, without much chance of resumption.

///

At home, Leah's room had been neat. Whether this was because her mother commanded it, or because John might look in on it, Leah was never entirely sure. Some might call the room arranged, others just tidy.

Still, Leah ventured forth each day in fresh attire, her unwrinkled, well-fitting sweaters fetching the most compliments of all.

What had happened here at college? she wondered. She brushed her teeth only every other day, squeezing the tube for every last little bit of paste because she had not gotten around to buying more. Clothes lay scattered on the floor as she put off visits to the laundromat and cleaners. Even the white rug had pizza stains. Occasionally, she just grew tired of feeling grubby and vowed to reform. Which she did, but because hygiene and cleaning in college are made for procrastination, her vows worked only halfway and for a while.

By February, Leah hardly left her room, sentenced there by term papers more than the weather. Indoors made her feel all mind and no body, so useless had that physical vessel become. She was tapping out thoughts on the efficacy of executive orders, wondering what use she would ever make of all this knowledge, musing idly that she wanted a pet curled at her feet, when Katie paid her promised visit.

"You look like an over-caffeinated wreck, Leah."

The two women had become friends of a sort, now that they weren't in class together every day, though their affection was often hard to discern. Leah had not encouraged this visit, this unwelcome reminder of the plain origins she'd left behind.

"What a surprise, Katie, to find you speaking your mind. 'Katie Overdrive' they used to call you."

"Leah Richards used to be your name. Now who are you?"

"Back off," Leah warned.

"No!" came the reply. "Leah, you hardly ever set foot in Woodson these days or bother to check on old friends when you do. People say your nose is way up in the air and—"

"Damn it," Leah shouted at the one person who could make her curse. "Just by doing nothing more than going to Harvard, just by being here, folks back home say I'm a snob. And what do you suppose people at Harvard say—that just by being from Woodson, which they've barely heard of, I'm some kind of country hick. What in hell am I supposed to do? Get out of here before I kick you out."

Katie was so startled at Leah's cursing that she broke out in laughter. "You're a good cusser when you put your mind to it."

"Well, if you want to learn, I charge for lessons."

That's the way it went with the two of them. Strong words, no grudges; so, they began to plan the evening. Katie had insisted on a nice restaurant and movie, though Leah protested she could not afford the time. Katie had chatted on about this person and that place, all of little relevance to Leah now.

Katie herself was studying to be an accountant, "in Woodson of course."

Of course, Leah thought uncharitably, as she imagined walls closing in on Katie's world.

Still, Leah admitted, the visit could have been much worse. Friends are not always the ones you most want to see, but the ones that keep up with you, she thought. She had not wanted Katie to come, but she was in no hurry to see her go.

With Hank and Leah off at college, Ellen was left at home with her mother—the ever-practical, driven parent, with no one nearby to turn off the ignition—and it was not going well. The daughter was adept at tuning the parent out.

Had it not been for their neighbors, the Fergusons, things would have been far worse. Jim came over each Saturday to mow the lawn. He was Woodson's best. Perfect edging, no gouges, he could have earned a living at landscaping were he not a dentist. He was also by nature a listener, which made Ellen miss her father all the more.

Nancy came over with baked goods and meatloaf. Meatloaf can be made many ways, but Nancy's ingredients were infused with love and patience and brought Ellen and her mother a rare moment of accord.

The Fergusons had loved Frank Richards, and now they offered to take Ellen on a tour of colleges—a chance to escape home, which Ellen readily accepted.

Still, the situation deteriorated. A very high-strung mother and laid-back daughter, Jim explained in a phone call to Leah. Could she come back home one weekend and at least try to straighten matters out?

Leah complied, although she could hardly have been a less suitable mediator at this point in her life. She thought it all an inconvenient interruption. She was not prepared to be dragged back in time.

"Ellen," said Leah as they lunched on two Big Macs, "we both need to understand what Mom's going through." Ellen liked fast food, especially on weekends, and Leah had agreed to a McDonald's visit.

"Imagine how you'd feel," Leah continued, "if you'd lost the person who meant the most in the world to you. We really need to try and help her out."

"I know all that," replied her sister, "but Mom's so controlling. I mean every little thing. 'Who was that you were calling? Clean out your closet.' And sometimes you sound just like she does. I don't need two mothers. I'm a high school senior. Get that? A senior! I may not make the best grades in town, but I'm old enough to know what I want, which is to be left alone to be myself."

The whole situation struck Leah as absolutely impossible, what with her mother complaining constantly that Ellen needed to "grow up." The two of them were never meant to be alone together under the same roof.

Leah heard, however, from both her mother and sister what the Fergusons had done since her father's death. She went over several times to thank them. It was what anyone would do, they said. But it had been a revelatory moment, something she had almost forgotten. Two nice people, bestowing such kindness on her family. And not a thing in it for them.

///

Changes came to Woodson, but not precipitously, and the town was always able to knit together present and past in a way few other places could.

Alumni Weekend at Woodson High in early May was one such occasion. Hank came because he was still regaled for his football exploits. Ellen came because as a Woodson senior, she felt she should. Margaret Richards came, because she needed something, anything, to arrange. Gloria came in order to convince people she was not Gloria. Katie came to catch up.

Many of those milling about had seen each other on Friday and would again on Monday. Introductions were a lost art. There was the traditional choice between tuna and chicken salad. Those feasting laughed anew over the horrendous sketch Billy Wilson had drawn, way back when, of Mr. Carson, as the oral history of Woodson High was replenished with annual repetition.

John came because he had a soft spot for Woodson High and because he never entirely knew whom he might meet there. His heart raced. He wanted to run into Leah. No, he did not. Yes; no. No! The unbearable nervousness at the thought she might be bringing a guest.

"People are asking about you," Ellen phoned her sister.

"Like who?"

Ellen released a few names.

"Is that all?" Leah said.

"Well, you never know," Ellen teased. "By the way, we're going rafting Sunday."

That changed Leah's mind, and she made plans to come home. She had always loved the river, the feel of the paddle, the cool of the spray. And Sunday promised to be a beautiful day.

The experience was all that she remembered from Alumni Weekend. Except that John was not beside her, as he used to be.

He had not seen Leah on Saturday and went back to Penn State late that day.

But not before, Leah heard, organizing a soccer game for lower formers and assisting Mrs. Whiting with her wheelchair.

"Stroller and wheelchair," John once said. "Beginnings and ends need care."

What other guy would have made that observation? Leah had wondered at the time.

///

It dawned slowly on Leah that she might not be a summa at Harvard, or even a mere magna, and the recognition ironically softened her heart a bit toward Woodson. Could she learn to savor its good moments? Or had she, in her more hurried Harvard moods, bathed in deceptive nostalgia Woodson's slower pace?

She was coming into balance, she thought. She wanted that one-half of herself that was Harvard and the one-half that was Woodson. Or was it two-thirds Harvard? Which fraction belonged to which place? Who was to know?

It was a shame, she thought, that the two places were so different. Little overlap between them. It seemed to force on her a choice she did not wish to make. Not yet, anyway. She could not get her friends in one place to understand the other. Worse still, there was no desire to try. No one at Harvard ever really inquired about Woodson. As for Harvard, her Woodson friends could care less. It got so she could see someone and tell from which sort of place they came. It wasn't just hair length or dress or even speech, but that indefinable thing called bearing. Call it stereotyping, but location stamped upon some a certain practical, hands-on look, upon others the serious self-regard that ambition and accomplishment can bring.

So it was that a long dinner with self-important blowhards caused Leah to think of John once more. John was Woodson; Woodson, in turn, was John. She had not met anyone quite like him at Harvard; his empathy could calm the waters around him and bring her back to shore. But then again, he was not a future governor or millionaire, and Leah was not above such thoughts.

At any rate, it was all idle musing, she supposed. John's dark hair was impossibly handsome. Six feet and two inches, he could sweep any woman off her feet. He'd doubtless met someone at Penn State, and when they'd ventured forth from Woodson, there seemed the unspoken recognition that theirs were the kind of futures that left the old familiarities behind.

John, too, was sure of that. Leah was ambitious; she was outpacing him; a brilliance like hers would find him boring over time. But somehow, she transferred energy and drive to him; she had made him a gift of her mind; she placed a compass in his hand without which he floundered and was uncertain where to go.

Well, what did it matter? She had met someone at Harvard. They had not kept in touch and learned of one another mostly through fragments of hearsay. Little snippets that got them wondering. First Leah then John had thought of picking up the phone, but they never did. Was it not better to wonder than to know?

Then the news came: Margaret Richards had suffered a stroke.

///

The two sisters rushed to their mother's side. It was worse than feared: left side paralysis, loss of acuity, slurred speech. Ellen cried openly when she saw her mother; Leah felt tears would only add to her parent's distress.

"You have to take this in stages," the nurse had said. "You can't do it all at once." Leah figured she had said it a thousand times before.

They took her back to a home they barely recognized. A dark, lonely place into which their father had long ago brought love, the children the peculiar joys of sibling chaos. Leah missed what she never thought she would—her mother's scolding presence that seemed to whisk from room to room, wherever the three young Richards children happened to be.

"There now, can you move your left arm?" said the therapist. "Can I help?" And the sisters thought they once saw movement, but it was wishful vision. There was none.

"What can we do?" so many asked. There were foodstuffs, and the Fergusons pitched in constantly. Their Woodson classmates had taken up a collection. But the insurance and their family's modest savings would not begin to pay for round-the-clock care.

"It's the suddenness of it all," Leah confided to Nancy Ferguson. "Lots of things you can prepare for. Strokes hit like a lightning bolt at night."

///

One day, an unexpected check arrived in the mail. Five hundred dollars. From John. "Leah," the letter read, "I am so sorry. Hope this will help with your mom."

Two weeks later, another check arrived in the same amount. This time, Leah got in her car and headed for Penn State.

The sky was undecided, and Leah, too, did not know what to think. She had heard Penn State was huge, and entering large spaces all by herself and not knowing what to expect was, well, unsettling. The bigness of the campus nearly capsized her. She had to make multiple rounds of inquiries to track him down. She could have called his cell, assuming after all this time that his number was the same, but what she really wanted was for the meeting to be a surprise.

"Hello, John," she said finally. He was waiting tables at a steakhouse in town.

"Leah Richards." The stacked dishes wobbled on his forearm.

"Filet, medium rare," she managed to stammer.

And when the steak was eaten and the last unsurprising customer had departed, the two sat down.

"Do you actually like this?" Leah asked.

"You mean the waiting? I don't suppose it's so bad."

"It can't be fun."

"It depends. There's always the tension with the kitchen. Some of the customers don't know you exist. Others, nothing suits. Some nights good tips, nice people."

"All this standing up. What about your knees?"

"Well, it's more your back. But nothing a good night's sleep can't cure."

Their words went on fumbling.

"John," Leah said finally. "Why are you doing this? This job? You aren't on scholarship. You don't have loans."

He paused, eternally, in Leah's view, before leaping.

"Leah, the Richards have always been my family. My own folks are okay in their way, but, as I've often told you, they're cold."

"But what does that have to do with waiting tables?"

"Well, when I heard about your mother, I was devastated. I know she always thought of me as a papist, but I felt she was coming around. And I was getting to like her too.

"Anyway, when I heard the news, I wanted so much to do something. But here I was at Penn State, a bit distant. And if I went back to Woodson, I couldn't so much as see your mom. Knowing her, she had her dignity. Particularly with a man."

Leah had never listened more intently.

"But what I could do was wait these tables. And send my earnings along to you. I know what a drain these things are on family finances. My uncle was bedridden for years, and it really pinched."

"I can't let you do this, John," Leah said through tears.

"I have to do it, Leah. My life needs a reason."

There was so much to talk about, no end of things to say. But that night was spent discussing care for Leah's mother, how best to make do.

///

Somehow, they all patched it together. Three caregivers; Mrs. Richards would not spend a moment in the house by herself. Nancy Ferguson came in to cook and do laundry. Jim saw to the yard and house repairs. Ellen came down from Dickinson, where she was now attending college. Self-conscious at first that Dickinson was not Harvard or Penn State, Ellen had come to appreciate its smaller size and to recognize it as a happy fit. Much closer to Woodson than Leah, Ellen kept her older sister up to date. Leah, scrambling with term papers, came down as often as she could. John, also in his last semester, kept sending funds and would somehow find what needed doing whenever he was back in town.

Leah was being pushed into adulthood faster than she was ready to go. Parents, she thought, the good ones anyway, were such an umbrella. You expect them to shelter you until you're at least forty or so. To have someone older and wiser or at least wealthier to catch you if you stumble and fall. Now here she was without cover or shelter, and the thought so unsettled her that she did what she had resolved never to do even when her father passed: see a therapist.

People swore by Dr. Davis with his gentle mien and clean white coat. Sometimes they had to wait a bit in the reception area, as the good doctor was reluctant to terminate a session just because its scheduled time was up. Leah avoided the problem by booking her appointment early in the day. She stepped into his office with its framed diploma and recognitions, its pictures of presentations, thinking he might help.

And in a way he did. "Leah," he said, "I've known you since you were a little girl. If there's anyone in all of Woodson who could work through this rough patch, it's you. I just want you to know you're not alone. I'm always here if you need me. I'll script you a mild sedative anytime you wish, but just talking things through and opening yourself up can sometimes beat any medication."

Leah left feeling more determined. She wouldn't, at least for now, take medication. "You will or you won't. You do or you don't." Her mother made the old saying unforgettable.

It became clear to Leah that her mother would always be an invalid. Her mother did not want her friends to see her in her present state. She was experiencing the weakness in her limbs that those who'd never had a stroke could not describe. Leah watched her parent living ever deeper inside her illness. There was little talk or inquiry of anyone else.

Neither Leah nor John knew where they stood with one another. They were focused on the task at hand.

"Mrs. Watson would make a good caretaker, don't you think?" She needed his judgment on whom to hire.

"Agreed. The references are good. A sweet manner. Won't come unhinged by your mom's demands."

Was there less teenage stardust in her eyes? Leah wondered. Or more gratitude? What did it matter? There was no one else to turn to.

Hank was posted to Fort Campbell, on the Kentucky-Tennessee border. For Second Lieutenant Richards, it was a dream come true. The fort was home to the 101st Airborne Division, the "Screaming Eagles," the elite of the elite, the most mobile of the Army's light infantry divisions, trained for air assaults.

Hank loved the pomp and circumstance. That rank on his Class A uniform, the salutes coming his way even as a junior officer, were really something. But he was far more than a parade ground soldier; he could crawl through sand and grit with the best.

Hank sent smiling pictures home to cheer his mother up.

Leah wondered if her brother had any sense of the full gravity of the situation, but she was happy for him. And proud too. Hank Richards, American warrior, and no one was going to challenge that.

Still, through it all, Hank was a source of worry for his sister if only because he worried so little about himself. "Hank's all motion, no reflection. Is that any way to live?"

"I love your green-blue blouse," John said.

"You're infuriating, John. I try to ask a serious question, and guys just fixate on physical appearance."

"I'm sorry, Leah. What was it you asked?"

"I wanted to know whether the unreflective life is any way to live."

"Hank just loves being Hank. Isn't that your answer?"

"But he lives so totally in the moment."

"So he does. To the extent he even bothers to think ahead at all, he probably shrugs and thinks eternity will take care of itself."

Leah thought the right relationship would help stabilize Hank. But finding the right person would be a daunting challenge, and Hank was not one to be open to suggestion. The girls always had an eye for Hank, but Leah thought Katie was a bit too keen. "You might at least say hi to Katie when you're next on leave," Leah wrote her brother, knowing full well that Katie was the last thing on Hank's mind. But at least if Katie mentioned Hank, Leah could say she'd tried.

John had a small worry of his own. He'd sat in the Woodson stands with Leah and watched Hank's gridiron deeds, and he now sensed he might soon hear of her brother's wartime heroics too. Against Hank's machismo, John worried he'd always come off second best in Leah's eyes. He genuinely liked and respected Hank, they'd always gotten on well, but they were as different as night and day.

He needn't have worried. Hank was just the kind of person Leah wanted as a brother. But he introduced her as "my egghead sister," a term that steamed Leah but one that John always regarded as a compliment. And Hank could never in a million years have grasped the situation that now confronted her and John. "John, I'll never be able to thank you enough," Leah said, as she put her head on the shoulder of her partner in her mother's care. "Words can't express it, so let's just sit quietly."

///

They returned to Woodson after graduation. For John, the choice was simple; he liked the town. For Leah, not surprisingly, matters were more complicated. Those who return to small hometowns after college often make a tradeoff—accepting a ceiling on a career for the comfort of familiar surroundings.

Leah had no such choice. Law school would have to wait. It was inconceivable for her to be anywhere but Woodson, given her mother's condition. No daughter would abandon a parent in such straits. Still, she wondered, would a son be expected to put his career similarly on hold? Hank wasn't putting his life off. Was continuing with John also a compromise? She thought not. She needed him. He understood her. Her relationships with more ambitious men had crashed and burned.

John had finally settled on an English literature major at Penn State, had taken the requisite education courses, and decided he wanted to teach. Upon returning to Woodson, he became a teacher at Prentis Middle School, the dreaded time where students would be more occupied with puberty than literature. But there was a special place in heaven for middle school teachers, people said, and this was at least a start.

John was no complainer, but the middle school zoo would tax the patience of a saint. Twenty-four was too large a class, and the teaching assistants were only part-time. A peanut butter sandwich once hit him in the back of the neck. It was, the student swore by way of apology, aimed at someone else. It would cost too much, the principal explained, to give the teachers a duty-free lunch.

"And this is education?" Leah would ask.

"Why, yes, because every so often someone's face comes alive with recognition, and you say to yourself, well that's a start."

Leah for her part was consumed with her mother's comfort. She planted window boxes of petunias for her mother to see. Purple and white: her mother's favorite combination. She and John set up an aquarium with two angel fish swimming slowly, dreamily along to give her mother peace. The room was kept quiet. The noise on which Margaret Richards once thrived now seemed to give her pain.

The days could be dispiriting. Leah would walk in, gaze gently at her dozing parent, and wonder whether this version of her mother could still extract small pleasures from her surroundings or whether she had reached that stage in life that longs only for the oblivion of death. "Mother," she would say softly, "it's me, Leah, and I love you." She had learned not to expect anything in response.

She worried, too, that she would wear John out with the repetition of dark thoughts. He did his best to lift her mood—and with some success. At Harvard, Leah had missed the outdoors. Back in Woodson, she took a job with Parks and Recreation. John reintroduced her to the full pleasures of outdoor life, the perfect release from her mother's confined state. He would plan hiking trips for the weekends—the Appalachian Trail passed through nearby Boiling Springs—often with a stay at a bed and breakfast or even a cabin or, more rarely, a tent. Leah learned to relish what she called their mountain banter.

"Your hair, so beautiful, it puts these hills to shame," he said.

"Altitude affects you," she laughed. "Let's go down where you can make more rational judgments. But wait." She was learning to love their *solitude à deux* on high.

They did go down to a little inn for the evening where he, as usual, let her choose the wine. A simple quaintness surrounded them.

Later she felt a lasting truth within as her softness sent him off to far, contented sleep.

///

Being back in Woodson, Leah had to admit, was not entirely bad. Lots of little things. The Safeway, she thought, was a first-rate grocery store. Its aisles were long, its shelves well stocked. Shopping there could even be a bit of an adventure if, that is, Leah wasn't rushed.

"Hm," Leah said as she consulted her checklist. Kleenex, paper towels, potatoes, head of broccoli, two percent milk. She was trying to run the most efficient route. Leah laughed as she approached the peanut butter. Last month, she had bought a jar of Skippy Creamy. John preferred crunchy, and he had pitched a fake fit.

Turning her bounteous cart into a crowded aisle, Leah stopped abruptly. There at the other end, staring intently at an array of breakfast cereals, was Gloria, whom she had scarcely seen since graduation. When another customer rounded the corner and reached out for the last giant-size box of Corn Pops, Gloria grasped the bright cardboard, apparently having suddenly made up her mind to wrest that particular box away from the competition and keep it for herself.

Corn Pops, Leah mused, a wholly inappropriate food for a grown woman. Did that mean Gloria was married? Had children? Or was it for a niece or nephew? No, not that. Gloria never did anything for other people.

The mystery of the danged cereal box had so piqued Leah's curiosity that she momentarily thought of greeting Gloria, until the remembrance of animosities past intruded, and Leah checked out hurriedly and unobserved.

"You'll never guess who I saw today," Leah said that evening to John, who was deep into a newspaper.

"No, too many possibilities, I never would."

"Gloria!"

"How did she look? I mean, seem."

"Well, her last remaining asset is wilting before our eyes."

"Honestly, Leah, Gloria always brings out the worst in you. Why not just forget her?"

"Not so easy. The fascination of the abomination, I suppose."

"Oh, for Pete's sake. What's happened to Gloria I hardly know. You and I have more to do these days than give her a moment's thought."

Of course, thought Leah, as John sank back into his paper. Whether present or long absent, the evilness of Gloria had always eluded guys.

The phone rang one night, and a breathless Ellen was on the other end. Ellen, as was her wont, danced around the real subject, enjoying the suspense.

"Ellen, why exactly are we having this conversation?" asked her purposeful sister.

The next moment Ellen announced she was getting engaged. She and Norman had met at Dickinson, and Ellen was enchanted, dangerously so.

"It's too soon," Leah said, startled at her parental tone.

"You haven't even met Norman," Ellen shot back.

"I don't need to. You're barely twenty," and, still in Leah's eyes, her cute, slightly playful, but wholly vulnerable little sister.

Leah sometimes thought John infuriatingly non-judgmental, but on this, they were solid. Still, he said, "We need to meet Norman" to have any hope of heading Ellen off from what could be a disastrous mistake.

"God," sighed Leah, "as if we don't have enough on our plates without this."

John could see Leah was frantic. "Stop pacing," he urged.

"Mom would be pacing, too, John. At twice my pace."

He watched her mind clicking as fast as her feet.

"I'm going to Dickinson, John. I'm going to shake her into sanity."

"And watch her elope the next day?"

Her agitation left him helpless. "Leah," he said finally, after putting on some soothing background music, "this seems like Ellen's rebellion."

"So?"

"So maybe we should just look completely nonchalant, almost as though we'd never heard the news. That might cool things off a bit."

"When was the last time I acted nonchalant about anything?"

At which point John turned off the music. He knew enough to know she had to be left to work it through.

After some thought, Leah sent John on a mission. "Talk Ellen out of this," she pleaded. "She won't listen to her big sister, but she might to you."

John agreed and met with Ellen. "We had some good discussions," he reported. "Talked it over on a long walk. Then again over Big Macs . . ."

But he had come back empty-handed.

///

Small towns have a way of becoming distinctive. At least this was the case in Central Pennsylvania. Woodson's Ten Miler was a major regional event, attracting as many as four hundred runners. Early October marked the last few days of apple harvest time, and a few of the remaining seasonal pickers had even entered the race. John and Leah always gave it a go, huffing and panting near the finish line, but their times never really broke the mid-eighties, and so they were subjected to the joshing of their mid-seventies friends.

The big news though was that Norman was coming for the barbeque and ribs picnic after the race. A nice setting, Leah thought. Woodson's hospitality would be on full display.

Ellen, too, was excited. She had reeled in a very big catch, a blue blood from Manhattan, and she was eager to bathe in her sister's adulation.

"Leah, this is Norman," Ellen beamed.

"Hello, Norman," said Leah in her nicest manner. He was altogether presentable, Leah thought, a little too much so.

"You can take off your tie," Leah laughed, struggling not to prejudge. "Here, let me give you one of our racing T-shirts you can take home as a souvenir."

"Norman doesn't need a T-shirt," Ellen interjected.

"Of course. It's always tricky, finding the right size."

"Let me introduce you to some of our friends," John suggested, responding to Leah's quiet plea for relief.

When the Fergusons came over, Leah explained all they had done after her father's death.

Norman listened politely and murmured "That's nice," before delving into an opportunity that awaited him in Manhattan.

Brushoffs all afternoon, Leah thought. But not everyone saw it that way.

"Such a new situation, Woodson, PA. Smalltown, USA. Can you believe how well he handled it?" Ellen gushed to her sister that evening.

///

After some discussion, Leah and John decided they should give Norman a second chance. They invited Ellen and Norman to Giovanni's, where they thought he might like the veal. It was the perfect setting to get to know Norman better than they could at a large event.

"Hello, hello," said the expansive Giovanni as he ushered the foursome to his most discreet table. He had brought the little restaurant up from nothing to the most prized eatery in town.

"And what may I bring you to drink?"

Norman asked for a wine that was not available. As for the atmosphere, the red-and-white checkered tablecloths had left Norman unimpressed.

John had warned Leah that small-town residents could be too quick to sense condescension, but this was no figment of Leah's imagination.

Norman talked of his trips to the Met—"the Metropolitan Opera," he clarified gratuitously for John and Leah. John stroked Leah's arm as she gripped the sides of her dining chair. And then the little present Norman had bought Ellen on Fifth Avenue—he wanted to give her something special, "Something she couldn't find around here."

Throughout the evening, he texted off and on—matters that couldn't wait. A painful silence descended on the veal. The disgust on Leah's face was no longer disguisable, which led to a unanimous decision to dispense with coffee and dessert.

Ellen was angry at how the evening had gone south.

"It's humiliating, isn't it, Leah, to have little sis marry first. You just can't stand not being first in *everything*."

At which point John pressed his Visa upon a stupefied Giovanni, and the couples sped their separate ways into the night.

///

John agreed. It had been a disastrous evening. "Except for one thing."

"You're kidding?" Leah looked up from her book.

"Ellen's out-of-character remark."

"You think it was really out of character? I don't mean to be harsh on my baby sister, but she's always had a chip on her shoulder about me. Like I expect her to live up to my expectations for myself."

John hesitated. "You don't . . ." He said it as a question and a statement.

Leah sat straight up. "No!" She snapped her book shut and slapped her knee. "I've only ever wanted her to set expectations for *herself* and to live up to *those*. She's far more capable than she realizes, and she could apply herself . . . well, anyway. We're getting off topic. You said her remark was the one good thing to come out of tonight?"

John smiled and nodded.

"Meaning?"

"Meaning," he said as he stepped behind her and rubbed her tense shoulders, "why wait?"

"I'm still not getting you," she said.

"You know, it's not foreordained that Ellen be first at the altar."

A moment of silence passed between them.

"What a way to back into a proposal," Leah laughed, eyes closed, rolling her neck and shoulders into his hands to deepen the massage.

John placed a hand on her chin and turned her face toward his. "I'm serious."

Her eyes flashed wide, and she searched his face for a hint of mischief. Finding none, she said with all her heart, "Yes!"

"Exactly what I was hoping you'd say." He smiled. "But with Leah Richards, you never know."

The proximity of the past year had been good to them. To be sure, there were short and snappish moments for which, Leah admitted, her impatience was the culprit. But they had made a team in the sense that together they got smoothly done all those little things in life that needed doing. They also developed what they called their post-midnight routine. When one of them got up to check something out or write something down or visit the bathroom, he or she would crawl back to bed murmuring a soft comment the sleeping partner would most like to hear.

And when Leah finally enrolled in nearby Dickinson Law School, John brought a common sense, real-life take to cases that her classmates had been missing. "You're only twenty-four, buster, but you've been around," she would say.

And Leah had helped him appreciate literature. For all her sharp intelligence, she had a sense of beauty and feeling that made the plays and poems and novels he taught come to life even more. "What's a sensitive soul like you doing in law school?" he would say.

"Did you ever think back in high school that we'd actually end up like this, John?"

"Not when you left me for Harvard." He chuckled.

"Who left whom?" she exclaimed, pretending shock.

He drew her to him. "The odds are all against high school sweethearts, but darned if I don't think we beat them."

///

Leah dropped into Giovanni's one afternoon, three p.m. to be exact. The hour right between the luncheon and dinner servings, when the maestro just might allow himself a moment off. There he sat, oddly out of character, wiping his brow until he spied Leah and jumped up: "I'm hoping these rumors I'm hearing are true," his voice boomed to the kitchen and beyond.

"It's true, Giovanni. It's true! We're getting married!"

"The perfect couple, and may Adriatic breezes bless your way."

"Our wedding dinner will be right here, Giovanni, with you!"

"Wonderful! Let's have a look at the menu."

"That's on you," Leah needled. "We've made our choice, you make yours."

"Phew! Such responsibility," he sighed with another mop to his forehead. "You know, Leah, I was feeling a bit down when you came in. But good customers remind me why I'm in this business. You could make a ninety-year-old chef feel sixty."

"Long ways to go before that." Leah laughed. "Where's my hug!"

One of the most fun things about getting married, she thought driving home, was telling people you were getting married. Giovanni was not her age nor from her background, but friendships form on a bridge, and that was that.

///

They planned a very small wedding. These ceremonies were for parents, they both felt, and Leah was certain her mother would never be able to attend. Then, too, they didn't want to upstage Ellen with something large. They would get married in John's Catholic church. They were both ecumenical in religious outlook, and the church did not become the issue it would have been had Margaret Richards been her active self. Mostly, however, they just wanted to get married and didn't much care how.

"No presents," the invitations said. But Leah gave John an early edition of Moby Dick, and John had Leah's Harvard diploma framed.

"The Gifts of the Magi," Leah proclaimed.

"I'd give that one no more than a 'B' in class," he laughed.

The arrangements jelled quickly, and why not, with a couple in love in charge. Katie was invited. Gloria was not. The Fergusons, whom they affectionately called their adopted parents, were to be on the front row. John's parents came, though even after all this time, Leah never quite knew how they felt about her. Hank was best man. Ellen was maid of honor. Norman wanted to come but couldn't, she explained. However, he had sent a nice gift.

The day was blue; Leah awoke excited but not jittery, so certain she was in what she wanted to do. It all unfolded as planned. St. Thomas Aquinas was bedecked with lilies, the ceremony blessed with the priest's benevolent smile. And afterward, as husband and wife, the joyous couple met a beaming Giovanni, who had reserved for the little wedding party an appropriately intimate side room.

The meal was Giovanni's best, course upon course, a feast. Everyone seemed to be snapping pictures of everyone else. A waiter tripped and broke some dishes, but the jovial guests jumped in to help clean up.

The toasts of course drifted far down memory lane. A guest suggested they sing the Woodson Song. "Nay," another shouted, but the tipsy "yeas" won out.

"I have but one fear," John said in his toast. "That I may lose my job. Our honeymoon is one from which I may never return."

To the surprise of all, Leah was speechless, once more the lovestruck senior at Woodson High.

///

There had been no shortage of suggestions for their honeymoon. A friend of John's mentioned Easter Island "where no one could ever find you." A friend of Leah's joked about Antarctica "so you can see the ice before it melts." Henry, who was a hiker, actually searched Himalayan base camps, but settled on Mount Kilimanjaro, because "I've heard that's quite doable."

All of which drove them to something quite conventional: England! Leah, because of its legal tradition; John, because of its literary heritage. John was rewarded when he saw in the British Museum an early illustration of Sir Thomas Gray's *Elegy Written in a Country Churchyard*.

"Do you think when he wrote that he knew it would become so famous?" Leah asked.

"Probably not," John said. "But his sense of self-satisfaction must have been great. Anyway, the elegy was to ordinary folks who never became famous. It always amuses me, Leah, that these kings and emperors, or presidents for that matter, wonder whether they will be legendary, which is all kind of silly because you never know how posterity will deal with anything."

They spent an evening in London on a "pub and play" routine. They saw any number of magnificent cathedrals with their endless scaffolding. "I guess nothing you construct is ever complete," Leah said.

"Right. Just look at all the potholes in Woodson."

And they made the obligatory trip to Buckingham Palace, which they both thought an oppressive place to live.

"The royals do, too, I suppose," said Leah. "Being human, they can't wait to escape to Windsor or, even better, Balmoral."

Finally, they rested several days in the Cotswolds, where they lamented that the soft, honey-colored limestone was so vulnerable to acid rainfall.

Then suddenly it dawned on them that they had barely scratched the surface, that their trip was nearly over, and that they never, ever wanted this, their one and only honeymoon, to end.

It was clear that Ellen was going ahead with it. She had not heeded the advice of those three years her senior, so a date was set.

Leah sensed that Ellen saw in Norman all the suavity and sophistication that was missing from Woodson life. As for Norman, if he absolutely had to get married in Woodson, he at least wanted his New York friends to set the tone for the occasion.

A small wedding would not do for either of them, so the planning commenced for something more than the family budget really allowed.

"Why Save-the-Date cards?" As Ellen's surrogate mother, Leah had been dragged into preparations for something she did not at all approve of.

To top it all off, Leah sensed Norman's parents wanted rather little to do with her. His mother referred to her repeatedly as "my dear" in a way that unmistakably denoted an inferior. "Really, my dear, we don't do it quite this way in Rye." She could not for the life of her figure why her son was marrying beneath him.

"John, it's your turn to cook," Leah instructed, "and don't just toss up last night's spaghetti."

"Never fear, it's your favorite: veal marsala."

She smiled for the first time in days. He knew her mood would improve with the detestable event behind.

And the dreaded day did arrive. Hank, who was pleased with Ellen's upward mobility, escorted her down the aisle.

John saw an event without any personal touch. It could have been anybody getting married—just fill in the blanks.

"It's a two-in-one wedding," he told his friend Henry.

"What's that mean?"

"It means nobody, absolutely nobody on the bride's side knows anybody on the groom's side and vice versa."

"So much for mutual friendships," Henry said.

The room looked as though Moses had just parted the Red Sea. It did not bode well. Henry whispered to John that he wanted to smush a piece of wedding cake into someone's face just to get the party off life-support.

"Well," John said to Leah afterward. "I'm just glad it's over."

"I'm just glad Mother and Dad didn't have to see it."

///

Not long after Ellen's wedding, Margaret Richards died. Her last years had not been good.

For Leah, sunset had always been a time of reflection, but especially on this occasion, when the end of the day coincided with the end of a life.

There had been much to annoy Leah about her mother. But she came slowly to realize that her mother's relentlessness propelled them all. And Leah's father was devoted to her mother, so she could hardly have been all bad. Leah hoped for both their sakes that her highly agitated parent had found peace.

"You know that in literature funeral days are often gloomy or damp."

"John, that's hardly helpful."

"Well, I was thinking of Yuri Zhivago, that little boy, during the funeral liturgy for his mother. Anyway, Leah, I'm sorry. You didn't need that. I just didn't want you to feel all by yourself in foul weather."

Leah knew he was trying to help. That, in her experience, it was often hard for men to say the right thing at a sad time. And she was fond of the way John wove literature into their lives.

They both agreed Mrs. Watson had been a good caretaker. Leah's mother had difficulty swallowing, and Mrs. Watson knew what soft foods she liked. Then, too, Mrs. Watson was a stickler for clean linens. Sheets were the last things one went to sleep with and the first things one woke up with, and Mrs. Watson changed her mother's every day.

Last caregivers, they both recognized, are sometimes discreetly obscured at funerals, perhaps because they are too grim a reminder of the deceased's final months and days. Mrs. Watson deserved better.

As it happened, the day of the funeral forged a compromise: overcast, but at least no rain. And Mrs. Watson sat with a grateful family. She, too, was relieved the suffering was at an end, but she was thankful she had brought her handkerchief.

Several days later, when the neighborly visits had subsided, Leah and John took a deep breath.

"It's a strange world," she said, "where a wedding is sadder than a funeral." She curled next to him in bed. His warmth came through to her, a contented moment at long last.

"You know, John, we haven't watched an hour of television in a long, long time. Crazy busy we've become. Your choice, sweetheart."

She passed him the remote.

"Hmm . . ." he smiled. "I think I have a different preference."

///

Being some distance from Woodson, Hank was content to leave family matters to his sisters. His mind was elsewhere, mainly on combat, and Woodson offered little of the adrenaline on which he thrived.

News comes suddenly in the Army, crashing in on months of routine. And the news was what Hank had been waiting for: the 101st Airborne was off to Iraq. "Details to follow," he emailed his sisters as he packed.

The dust and heat in Iraq were what everyone said: temperatures often over 100 degrees. The porta-potties were even hotter. They stank. The toilet paper had always run out or was wet from the power washing. Many soldiers had an intestinal bug or irritable bowel syndrome or the proverbial green-apple nasties, all boiling down in Hank's mind to nothing more than a damnable case of diarrhea. To avoid it, he brushed his teeth with bottled water—but to no avail.

They wore the same dull sand camo fatigues each day. They trained nonstop. Marksmanship; use of protective masks against chemical attacks; street by street, house to house, face to face fighting. Above all, strength and endurance. No coaches or refs to call time-out in battle.

No matter. It was what he had been living for. All his life, they said he was a Man of Action. A Man of Purpose. A Man who was meant to say, "Mission Accomplished." That mission, now, was to bring Iraq democracy. So, onward his division marched: mopping up Iraqi strongholds; taking then guarding airfields; clearing whole cities; heading ever north as far as Mosul. The shepherd boys; the lengthy buttoned-up robes of Iraqi men. Who to trust? The training doesn't teach you. Then moments of triumph. Hank was not, to his dismay, at the shooting of Saddam's two sons, Qusay and Uday Hussein. But the fierce firefight was one in which all the troops took pride.

Back home, everyone knew that Hank was in the thick of it. Small-town America is nothing if not patriotic. The sisters were peppered by admiring questioners. Flags bedecked every store on Main Street. Woodson, Pennsylvania, glowed once more with pride.

CHAPTER

8

Upon graduation from law school at Dickinson, Leah took a job with a small Woodson firm, Hinkle, Smith, and Van Beek. Actually, with eight attorneys, it was one of Woodson's two largest. Leah's chief interest was criminal defense, but because so many cases were handled by public defenders, she supplemented her criminal caseload with commercial real estate work.

"James," she said to one of her clients charged with bank robbery, "the jury will clobber you with that story. They're good people here in Woodson, but it's not a good courtroom for someone in your situation to be."

She thought her job was to be frank. Going to trial was more glamorous perhaps, but acquittals were rare, and the best she could often do for those she represented was to bargain down the prison time.

Leah found criminal suspects a curious lot, some of them grateful, others wary, still others furious she hadn't gotten them probation. John noticed the job played havoc with her moods. Sometimes she came home sympathetic to the hard lives her clients led; other times she was appalled by the sheer cruelty they'd shown; still other days discouraged by the dwindling hope of redemption for those who'd made one bad mistake. "They'll probably never make it back," she confessed to her husband. "Who'll want to take them on?"

Then there were the white-collar scam artists "who ought to know better. What's their excuse?"

"Leah," John would say after hearing all this and seeing her worn down at the end of a day, "what keeps you going?"

"Well, even Attila the Hun deserves a lawyer. But every once in a while, I can save a decent kid from falling into the prison pit. Give him a chance. Whether he'll take it, I may never know."

Sometimes, after discussing these misfortunes, they felt very lucky, their own glass of life more than half-full.

But practicing law could be a grind. "That's why it's important to have a good husband," she sighed. "Someone who loves you even in a state of fatigue."

"Still can't understand why a Harvard grad would choose me," he said, half-seriously.

"It's the sheer physicality of you, John. You could have married the Queen of Sheba."

"It's the sheer cerebrality of you, Leah. Einstein would have found you scintillating."

"Yeah, sure; yeah, sure." They both laughed. And with that, harmony took hold, and the dark in due course brought its peace.

///

Leah and John both became fond of the Hinkles. Robert Hinkle, in his mid-fifties, was the managing partner at the firm. Leah found him a mild and fair man, too subdued, perhaps, to be a big city rainmaker, but for Woodson, a perfect hand in glove. His wife, Ginni, had a bit more sparkle, and together they made wonderful companions.

They were the kind of folks who grew on you. Leah may have under-estimated Mr. Hinkle at first, but not for long. He had sound judgment and erudition wrapped in modesty, and he saw law not as an object of reverence, but as an instrument of social benefit.

"To live in a place like Woodson," he said when the four of them went out to dinner one evening, "you have to be content with not being famous. Or even prominent. You probably won't be lionized at the state bar. At any political or professional gathering, for that matter. Philadelphia, Pittsburgh, and, yes, even Harrisburg, will suck all the oxygen out of the room. The small townships don't really count for much these days."

He said it without rancor, in the manner of a man at peace with himself.

"But how do you manage to quiet ambition," Leah had asked. "It's always knocking on your inner door."

The dinner had found Mr. Hinkle in a pensive mood. He took his time with each course. "I don't know that you ever completely quiet it," he said. "You can tell yourself that fame is fleeting, that the tumult and the shouting die, that sort of stuff. But that doesn't really do it for me."

"What does?" Leah wanted to know.

"Well what, finally, do you want your life to be measured by? And there's really only one good answer to that. It's how you treated those who crossed your way."

It had been a nice dinner. Woodson, John said afterward was like the play *Our Town*. Grover's Corner, New Hampshire. It gave you the chance, if you took it, to savor each day. "It's a perfectly ordinary observation, I admit, but that's the point. Ordinary is mercifully what life mostly is."

"You should have told that to Mr. Hinkle. He would have liked it."

"Oh, I don't want to go embarrassing you with another one of my third-grade literary allusions," he laughed. "So corny. The critics would dismiss me out of hand."

"Nonsense. You know I love your literary side. Books speak right to you, John. Tell you what's real."

"Well, I wasn't going to sit there tonight and interrupt your boss, Leah. Besides, Mr. Hinkle is a wise man."

And lucky, too, Leah mused. He and John. So much contentment. Leah, too, cherished her Woodson half as she drifted to sleep, knowing all the while that tomorrow the knocking would begin anew.

///

Finally, at long last, it seemed, the good news came. The superintendent, besieged by troubles all day, had taken delight in delivering it. For several years, John had done his stint at the middle school, and now he was to leave Prentis for a job teaching English at Woodson High.

It felt almost like Christmas; he could not wait to bring his wife the present of good news.

His face lit up the doorway. Leah knew how much it meant to him, and she gave him her biggest hug. It meant onward and upward to her, the things she wanted for her husband.

"John, you'll now be able to take graduate courses, get your master's or even doctorate, write the short stories or novels I know you have in you, all sorts of possibilities. Maybe even higher ed."

"Hold on! I just want to teach kids how to write. And to appreciate good writing. And life through great literature. I know full well my insights can be trite. But so what? Trite can be true. Anyway, you can't do a thing in middle school. High school, you've at least got more of a shot."

He wasn't through. "Leah, my dear, right now, please be a little more of a Frank and a little less of a Margaret. Not that I didn't love them both."

"Of course, sweetheart." Leah pulled back. She knew right away that she had stepped on this, his big day. "I'm so proud of you, honey," she whispered. "No takeout tonight." She set about preparing his favorite dinner. As John would say, it's all about acceptance. You can't make people other than what they are.

CHAPTER

9

The news they feared would come had arrived. Hank had been wounded, and badly. It was not clear if he would live.

A bomb in a house on the outskirts of Ramadi. A home thought to be friendly that was anything but.

He was rushed to a field hospital, his uniform soaked in blood, and from there to Landstuhl Regional Medical Center in Germany. Landstuhl would do what it could.

The two sisters were frantic. The reports were sketchy. Was it that the doctors didn't know or wouldn't tell?

The prognosis was guarded, so much so that Leah suspected the worst. "Come on, Hank," she would say through clenched teeth as if pulling for him from the football stands.

Leah and Ellen wanted to jump on a plane. "Doubt he would recognize anyone," the doctors warned. "Most of the time he is delirious."

///

The next ten days were the longest of their lives. It was all confusion. Hank didn't know where he was. The sisters didn't how he was doing. Leah obsessed about infection.

John was as aggrieved as any family member. He and Leah tried to cope in the only way they knew how—by losing themselves in one another.

Food supports many a marital relationship, and John knew Leah's tastes perfectly. She had acquired a fondness for Indian food at Harvard, and John now drove the seven miles outside Woodson to get her chicken tandoori and lamb biryani.

Leah for her part renewed her request that John teach Emily Dickinson in his junior English class.

"The guys," he cautioned, "wouldn't take to a female voice, at least not this one. Too tame."

"We could do with a little more tameness now," she replied. "And a little less war."

"Fair enough, sweetheart." Emily Dickinson's importance suddenly came home to him. "I'll give it a try."

At least, Leah told herself, I'll always have him.

///

Hank's condition improved from dire to critical to serious. He was flown stateside and now looked as though he might pull through. But what would his new life look like? He had lost a finger, and far worse, his right leg. The bomb had shredded it beyond repair. The athlete was now an amputee.

At Walter Reed, Hank was labeled "AK," for "above the knee." A prosthetic leg would have to be designed, joined, and fitted to the stump that remained of Hank's limb. Only the right length, bend, and socket would do. Hank would have to learn a whole new way of walking, one that required more effort because the new leg lacked the control provided by the old knee.

And Hank himself? A sound mind in a sound body, as the saying goes. Hank had always relied on his body, the physical feats he would forever perform for victory and glory. What use would he be now? Leah, John, and Ellen traveled to Washington DC to console him. "Legs," Hank sobbed as the full weight of his condition came down upon him. "Infantrymen need legs. Running backs need legs."

The two sisters and John talked with the team: doctors, psychiatrists, physical therapists, occupational specialists. They said what Leah and John predicted they would say. Ups and downs ahead. Uncomfortable stares at every street corner. A massive adjustment. This would take time.

And they would have a very impatient patient on their hands.

///

The goodness of next-door neighbors doesn't figure into the list price of real estate, but it should. Jim and Nancy Ferguson were one of the big reasons Leah and John decided to remain in her parents' house after her mother and father had passed.

Despite the friendly company in the neighborhood, not all of the local nostalgia was comforting. The house was haunted, not by a ghost, but by the personalities of furniture. The happy playful rugs of childhood; the sad declining window at which her mother sat. Quick, unexpected stabs of memory from simple trinkets, bracelets, cameos, and small vases. Why wouldn't they stop?

"Leah," Nancy said, "you haven't drawn a breath in weeks."

Visiting Nancy's home was a relief. It was a mild afternoon, so they sat in the deck chairs on the Fergusons' back patio.

"Sometimes it seems like nothing ever changes in a small town like Woodson," Leah commented. Nancy leaned back and closed her eyes, nodding. Leah continued, "But still . . . change seeps in. Look at these massive trees in your yard. They were always large, even when we were kids, but they're bigger now. Different. And we hardly noticed it happening." Leah sighed. "The shade is nice though." She, too, leaned back into her chair. "Do you miss being able to grow the beautiful, colorful flowers you used to plant back here?"

"Not really," she replied. "These two oaks have gotten so large that they don't let in much sunlight. So, I took to ferns. Out of necessity at first. But then I came to like them. Given good shade and moisture, they are really self-sufficient. Not demanding or high-maintenance like a man or a pet."

The two women smiled in mutual understanding but were forced finally to concede that husbands had virtues ferns did not. "Though I must say," Nancy added, showing Leah her northern maidenhair, "there are few things quite so beautiful as a healthy green fern plant."

Nancy was half a generation ahead of Leah. Old enough to impart wisdom. Young enough to catch upcoming trends and tastes. Leah could bring up any subject.

"Hank comes home tomorrow."

"How's he doing?"

"It's slow," Leah admitted. "I really don't know what I'm going to do with him. John's always a big help with the guy-to-guy stuff. He and Hank are real different, but they've always gotten along."

"It's hard to know, I suppose, how he'll react to anything," Nancy mused.

"That's right." Leah hadn't the slightest idea whether boyhood memories would be comforting to Hank or a poignant reminder of his present diminished state.

"Will you take him to Gettysburg?" Nancy asked. "Hank used to romp all over that place."

That's the problem, Leah thought. Would he still love those old statues and cannons and Cemetery Ridge and Little Round Top? The thought of tromping corps and battalions? Or would the whole scene bring back the horror of that moment in Iraq?

"I don't know, Nancy. What would you do?"

"You have to leave it to Hank. Offer, don't press. One thing," Nancy added, as Leah stood to leave. "Hank won't want to be hovered over. We women have to watch that."

"It's hard," Leah confessed. "No one wants to hover. But you can't let a brother suffer from sisterly neglect."

Nancy wrapped Leah in a firm hug, and Leah soaked up every ounce of support she could from that embrace before heading home.

///

Hank, when he arrived, was just flat. He didn't ask about anyone or anything. Leah had no idea what he was thinking, and he wasn't going to share himself with anyone, at least not right away. Visitors came, some of whom he seemed happy enough to see, others whose aimless chatter got on his nerves.

A pro football player Hank admired, a former Philadelphia Eagles linebacker, sent Hank an autographed football, which he put on the coffee table in the living room where he watched the games. That football was too valuable to scuff up, so Leah gave him others to hold because he loved the feel of the leather.

Hank took to watching mysteries. "Why don't they have crimes besides murder?" Leah asked.

"How boring would that be," he replied.

The main challenge was to make Hank less homebound. How to get him out in public and not have him self-conscious? Katie would help with that, Leah thought. She was not self-conscious about anything.

News came that Hank had been awarded the Bronze Star.

"That's fabulous," John said. "It's real courage, Hank. You'll be driving before long, and you can put that on your license plate. When I see that on a tag, I immediately respect the driver."

At this, Hank became responsive. "Thanks, John." Then, he considered for a moment: "I've watched the Olympics for many, many years. The silver medal is awarded to second place, the bronze for third. Same thing in the Army. Silver Star higher than Bronze Star." After another moment, Hank nearly smiled. "But just taking the medal itself, I've always found bronze more handsome. Don't ask me why."

"Me too, Hank," said John. "Not overly showy. There's something very statesmanlike about bronze."

"Of course, speaking for my former self," said Hank, "I'd always go for gold."

"Leah, she's been bruised."

Ellen had come to John while visiting Woodson from New York. Her arm and cheek were darkish purple.

Ellen explained that she had fallen down some stairs. Quite a tumble. But her eyes did not meet John's, and he was not convinced.

They determined to get the full story. Leah invited Ellen to the annual Ten Miler. It was a safe bet that Norman, given his disinterest in Woodson, would not come.

"Ellen," John said softly, "I did not see that bruise around your eye on your last visit. Did you have another fall?"

"Yes, the stairs at our place are quite tricky and . . ." Ellen broke off sobbing in mid-sentence.

"Norman thinks I'm a housemaid or something. Because he has all this money, that I'm so lucky he even agreed to marry me, and when I'm too tired to do the dishes or laundry or clean house right at the very second he wants, he gets really mad and starts shouting and threatening, and lands a fist or two. I'm crying, 'Norman, it's a big house and I can't do it all.'"

John held her hand. He sensed there was more to come.

"One night was real bad. Norman had been drinking, and he was angry I had not impressed his friends at the club. So, he's screaming at me on the way home about learning manners and how to carry on an adult conversation and how I'm plain and dull and he won't take me to the club next time . . . when we get home, he's so worked up and shoves me into a corner like in some boxing match or something, and I throw up my hands like a shield and he keeps slugging till I just slump . . ."

John had never seen Leah so furious.

"Dear, sweet Ellen," she said, "don't you ever go near that man again. You stay right here with us. And tell him if he ever sets foot here it will be the last step he takes. And if he ever touches you again it will be the last thing he touches. And that if I ever see him again, no matter the consequences, I will shoot him on sight."

///

So it happened that Hank and Ellen came to live with Leah and John, and the family was reassembled, though not in a way their deceased parents would have wished. Leah and John were asked in a sense to become parents, Leah's two siblings each being in a very fragile state. Piled on top of two full-time jobs, it was exhausting them.

"And we don't even have children," she said.

John only smiled. "Not yet."

"John, with everything we have on our plate, how can you make that kind of suggestion? Totally off-key."

John had learned not to contest these sorts of things. "I have something I'd like to run by you, Leah," he said that evening after Hank and Ellen had retired.

"Shoot."

"Well, as you know, I'm teaching *Pride and Prejudice*, and I've come to the conclusion that Jane Austen was in love with Darcy herself."

"Come again, John?" Their relationship was such that they each seemed to take turns bringing the other back to earth.

"See, I think novelists can fall in love with one of their characters, and in this case, Jane Austen found happiness of a sort by recreating Darcy as her suitor and Elizabeth Bennet as herself."

"And the evidence for this? John, wake up! One can't fall in love with fictional characters. They're not real."

"They are and they aren't. Writing is a lonely business. The imagination yearns for companionship and, more than that, for love. Anyway, read the book."

"Okay," she said. "I'll read it for the *third* time," she replied, subtly reminding him that she was no stranger to literature herself. "In the meantime, I don't want you writing any novels. No telling what heroines are out there." She drew him close. "No novels," she repeated. "I want you all to myself."

///

Like the oak trees in Nancy Ferguson's yard, Woodson Township was changing in slow and subtle ways. A small Comfort Lodge had been built on its outskirts, a clean, economy-sized, express check-out sort of place. It was a source of pride for the town that such a fine organization had chosen to locate there. Leah, too, thought it a nice fit. Small colleges, Civil War battlefields, orchards, and the outdoors had brought trickles of tourists to the area. Katie tried to keep track of all the comings and goings, though even she did not know that Gloria had become one of the new inn's assistant managers.

And, truth be known, Gloria was proving a success, as her supervisor received compliments from guests on her pleasant, accommodating manner. "To Gloria Jackson, who represents our own special brand of service," read the plaque at the annual employee recognition banquet. "Comfort and value," Gloria remarked briefly to applause and smiles all around.

Alas, the maids would tell a different story.

"No excuses. No excuses."

"I'm sorry, Ms. Jackson. Several guests left right at check out, and a couple even stayed over."

"I said I wanted those rooms made up by two o'clock sharp."

"We tried, Ms. Jackson. Honestly, we did."

"You'd best do better than try next time, or I'll assign you twelve rooms instead of ten."

"Yes, ma'am."

No wonder I'm where I am and they're where they are, Gloria thought to herself. She lived alone, munching Corn Pops as she watched hours of television. She did not plan to stay in service forever. One day she hoped to stop catering to others and be catered to herself.

And when the TV and lights were turned off, Gloria nursed griev-ances in the dark, those recent and those from long, long ago. No little black book necessary; she had it all in her mind.

///

Even Woodson's apples were playing their part in its change. The apple pickers came in the fall, seasonally at first, but the larger orchards could use regular attention, so some of them remained. A few migrants had come to love Woodson, and over time they moved from their first odd jobs to manage restaurants, barber shops, a car dealership, and a small hardware store. Their arrival brought some tensions, and the occa-sional haggles over language, but all in all, Leah thought, it made for a livelier scene.

The hardware store owner had even offered Hank a job. He declined, but appreciatively, because he worried his missing leg might chase cus-tomers away.

"It's all in your mind, Hank," Leah would say. "People love you."

He was trying hard; Leah knew there was no quit in him. But it was clear he was struggling. He was walking, but awkwardly. Worse, he sensed himself an object of pity in the eyes of those who once cheered him from the stands. The therapists and counselors were well meaning but of limited help, one even suggesting he might be better off in a place where he had no past.

Still, he was slowly improving, and Leah could see it in his gait. And Hank had one dream job in mind—if he could just find the courage to apply for it. His old coach at Woodson was still on the job, and Hank wondered if he might need an assistant. He had tried to conceal his limp as he entered the office.

"I could start with the running backs, Coach. I still remember the plays."

Coach Ramsey was moved but not prepared to resolve the situation face-to-face. He needed time to think. A macho game, he concluded finally, made a disabled coach a risk.

"I am most appreciative of your interest in this position, Hank," his letter read, "but there were a number of other highly qualified applicants, and I'm afraid I've had to choose one of them. If I can recommend you for some other position, you know of course that I would be happy to do so."

Hank was crushed but not entirely surprised. He could have done the job and then some. But the coach, he learned later, was concerned that his able-bodied team might look down on someone less so.

///

Ellen, for her part, was doing better. Or at least bravely pretending that she was. The divorce had gone through, to her immense relief. Norman had no more interest in continuing the match than she did. Leah considered a civil suit against him, but she and Ellen thought it best, in the end, to leave this whole hideous chapter behind.

Ellen moved into her own apartment. No longer was she second fiddle and fourth wheel. Armed with her Dickinson degree, she joined a real estate agency in town where two of her classmates worked. Not long thereafter she got her license, and because she was likable and knew the area so well, she was able to earn a few commissions.

"My motto, Mrs. Harrison, is child plus one," Ellen said, meaning couples should buy a house with one more bedroom than they have children. "Because," she continued, "you never know when you'll have another child, or want to invite guests, or convert that extra bedroom to a study."

"I don't know," her client worried, "it still seems a bit of a stretch."

"Well, you're right to be cautious," Ellen agreed, "but when you buy it's for the future. Imagine you and your husband five years down the road. This place will hold its value. Its location and structure are the best."

She gave honest advice. Leah and John saw it as a real success story. Ellen even took them out to Giovanni's one night to celebrate a sale and as a quiet thank you for their support during her recovery from abuse. They were happy that Ellen's social-climbing days were through and that she now seemed to find value in the little things. They sometimes judged these things by how much their father would be pleased, and they couldn't imagine him being unimpressed with Ellen's progress.

The river was running strong. The weather was beckoning, and the rafting party set out: Leah and John, Hank and Ellen, Katie, and a friend of Ellen's from the agency. The white water was too tempting to pass up, and the whole trip had a delicious feel about it.

Hank had been improving, though slowly. The sisters were pleased he wanted to do the trip, and they were not about to discourage anything that would boost his morale. The rafters donned their jackets, and the current pushed the raft downriver. Leah felt happily suspended between water and sky.

Ellen reveled in the spray. "Stop squealing," Leah pleaded.

"Right," laughed Katie. "You're disturbing her reverie."

"I can't believe that fallen tree is still there," John said. "You'd think someone would have cleared it by now." The limbs created small eddies in the water and made a welcome resting place for frogs.

Ellen was pleased her friend was having such a good time and entering into the spirit of the occasion.

Suddenly, Hank's lifejacket flew before Leah's eyes. The boating party turned to see Hank hurl himself over the edge of the raft. "No, Hank!" screamed Leah, but too late.

He had swum the river as a teenager without a jacket when his parents weren't looking, and he would prove to all that he could do so now.

And for one shining moment he was the Hank Richards of old, the master of every obstacle posed by nature and man.

And for that second, it seemed he might make it and throw them all into admiration and disbelief, until he felt the current's unforgiving might.

"Help me! Help me!" he yelled.

Those left on the raft were dumbstruck.

"Help me! Help me!" The cries grew distant as Hank was swept toward the big rocks and the waterfall.

"Save him, John!" Leah shrieked to the only man left on the raft.

"Save him, John! You have two legs!"

John was struck by panic and then practicality. There was no way he could save Hank, and he might lose his own life trying. Leah made a lunge for the edge; John was consumed with holding her back and keeping her safe.

"Help me! Help me!" the party heard for the last time.

In the next instant, all became clear. Leah and Ellen sobbed, and the river ran preternaturally still.

///

A numbness settled over much of Woodson, where Hank was well known and fondly remembered; it seemed to the townsfolk that he had led a heroic life, though one immensely sad.

The team knelt on the field before the opening game of the Woodson season, praying for one whose early demise and wartime courage had made him nearly mythic, an example Coach Ramsey would unabashedly hold up to each new crop of players for years to come.

For those around him, Hank's drowning left a large wake.

Katie made of Hank and herself an item in death that bore no relationship to any reality in life. No matter. She would become the keeper of Hank's flame.

Gloria would have her long-awaited revenge for John's lack of interest. She had not been on the raft, but she was confident about what had happened there, and she let people know it. John all along had the chance to save Hank but let him drown out of envy—Hank had the machismo John had always desired.

Leah was inconsolable. She knew, in her more rational moments, that Hank was one damn fool to jump off the raft. She also knew that rescuing Hank may not have been impossible but that any chance of doing so was slim. Yet it was another thought that lingered. Had the circumstances been reversed, Leah knew Hank would have tried to rescue John. He would have given no thought to himself. Not even on one leg.

Ellen alone was non-judgmental, perhaps remembering John's unfailing kindness to her during her disastrous break-up with Norman. "Don't go blaming yourself," she told him. "Hank was headstrong. Hank always did whatever it was that Hank wanted to do."

John was shattered. He had lost a friend. Leah's words on the raft had seared him. People sought to blame Hank's death on anyone but Hank, and the onus of that day had somehow descended upon him. Hank, people said, had once risked his life to rescue Baby Jenny, but there was no one willing to risk themselves for him. John worried about being known forever around Woodson as "the man who had a chance to rescue Hank Richards." He would normally work through these things with Leah, but her own grief had locked her in.

So it happened that a few fleeting seconds on a raft would be hashed out for many years.

///

"Please hand me the plate."

John did as requested.

"Thank you."

Their communication, always the strength of their relationship, had been reduced to few and simple words.

The monosyllables continued for weeks. Irritability did not require sounds to surface.

John did not know where to turn. His friend Henry was great at discussing politics, investments, sports, and movies, but he dug a moat around personal matters, and John let it be.

Few people knew all that happened. The rafting party was a small one, and they mostly respected Leah's silence on the matter.

Leah threw herself into work. She increased her coffee intake and stretched her workday to remain at the office as long as possible. But those at work saw as little of her as John did at home. Her physical presence remained, but her personality vanished.

"Leah, you've been in shock," said Mr. Hinkle as he walked into her office. He had taken off his tie, which he almost never did.

Mr. Hinkle had become like a father. He was why she looked forward to work in the morning, and he was the one she peeped in on at the end of a day. Comforting as the ritual was, she couldn't shake the thought: The people you most admire are often the ones you want the most to be like, but for some reason, you just can't. Try as she might to be more like Mr. Hinkle, Leah knew she wasn't made that way.

"I'm sorry," she said to her boss. "I can't speak about it. I try, but I can't."

Mr. Hinkle took a seat. "I don't know exactly what happened on the river, Leah, but from all I've seen of him, your husband is a good, good man. Some people you just place big bets on, even if you don't see everything firsthand."

Mr. Hinkle was not one to lecture. "Leah, this work can wait until tomorrow or the next day. Why don't you pick your favorite place and take a walk? Sometimes the woods will show you the way."

Which they did.

"Maybe we should get a dog," she said to John when she came home.

"Like a Jack Russell?"

"You're kidding?" she said.

"Yes."

And after going through collies and shelties, and labs and spaniels, John let out his own "arf." "Maybe," he said to Leah, "we're just barking up the wrong tree."

"John, that's truly sick. Even for you."

"Someone said at school a while back that couples always needed to try a dog before they had a child. And maybe, for some, that's true."

"And for us?" Leah asked.

"Up to you. Takes two."

"John," she said at the end of the evening, "I've taken out every last ounce of grief on you. As much as I adored my brother, I could never in a million years marry anyone like him."

He laughed. "Incompatibility on steroids, I should think."

It would take time for them both to heal, but tonight was a beginning.

"I'll give thanks to God for keeping you in that raft," she said. "I couldn't bear to lose you, too."

Tuesday was the day that Jerry and Brigitte moved in.

The appearance of a moving van in a neighborhood can be a moment of high consternation. Leah was quite content with her street as it was. She walked it early in the morning to the same chorus of waves and greetings, while the same little Scottie yapped at her as she passed by. "I hope one day you'll come to like me, Priscilla," Leah called to the dog who had in her own way become such a part of Leah's cherished rounds. Now here was this van like some huge, hulking monster coming to disturb her peace.

"I suppose it's like an aquarium," she thought aloud. "The fish shudder at a newcomer in the tank."

Despite her apprehension, Leah could not quite contain her curiosity as the van unloaded its contents. Furniture she would never, ever allow in her own house. Loud, brash belongings clashing with the quiet, leafy reserve of her block.

The newcomers were on the opposite side of the Richards from the Fergusons, and already Leah was beyond irate.

"Have you seen her?" Leah asked her friend Nancy. "Gunk for makeup and those long, tacky turquoise nails."

"Him? He's a lout. Overweight," complained Leah, "and half the time his lower button isn't buttoned, treating the whole neighborhood to the exquisite sight of his navel."

Nancy couldn't stop laughing.

"It's not funny, Nancy."

"I'm sorry. I'm just glad I live one door down. But look at it this way, Leah. At least he doesn't have a motorcycle."

///

The next morning Leah emailed Nancy of her mistake. Jerry had parked his Harley, made in York, no less, and was carrying his helmet into a job interview.

Leah froze. The Hinkle firm shared the building with several other tenants, and surely Jerry would not be poaching on her last preserve.

Then, from the reception area, Leah heard an unmistakable belch.

"Mr. Hinkle, do you have a minute?" Leah said the second Jerry left. "There has to be some mistake. Just a courtesy interview or something."

"Leah, Jerry has about the highest grades in the history of the University of Pennsylvania Law School. And he wants the small-town life. Coming from a school where so many graduates head off to New York, that says something for him."

Leah could not believe her meticulously attired boss was sitting there defending Jerry. "You can't stick him anywhere near clients," she replied, explaining the situation in the neighborhood.

Leah felt defenseless. The most persuasive man she knew was now in possession of the most preposterous plan. But Mr. Hinkle had a way of easing people into things. His voice soothed the ears the way his office soothed the eyes. He was the kind of counselor clients sought for reassurance, not adventure. The soft blues of his walls offered no hint of a surprise. So why this of all things! Jerry seemed the last man on earth Leah's revered boss would want nearby.

"Jerry's a good soul," he explained. "Not a mean bone in his body. Plenty odd, I'll grant you. But being odd is very different from being mean. And besides, I don't want someone that brilliant working for a competitor."

"So, where's his office going to be?"

"As far away from yours as I can make it," he chuckled. "He'll start out as a back-room guy. I'm appealing to your better angels, Leah. Let's give him a chance."

John also was incredulous when Leah told him that evening. They felt invaded as if by locusts.

Nancy, too, was no longer laughing. Jerry's lawn was uncut and the trash left about. "Five doors down from Dogpatch," Nancy said, "would not be enough."

///

A man stopped by the office a few weeks later. Leah had not seen him for years.

"William, please sit down," she said when she saw he was still standing. "We've been through a lot together, so make yourself comfortable. What are you doing these days?"

It was all coming back to her. She had begged and pleaded with the judge to give him probation. A battered childhood, teen years caught up in gang wars, and yet the hopeful letters from former teachers and counselors justified a leap of faith.

He would never, William swore to the judge, repeat the brutal assault. Even Leah herself was doubtful. "But there is this glimmer of good in him," she kept repeating to John, as if trying to reassure herself.

"I just came by to thank you," William now said.

"Fill me in."

"So, I got a job with a moving company. I guess they thought a muscle-bound black man could move anything. But no matter. It was a job."

"Well, how did it go?"

"Harder than you might think. Loading boxes on the van was the easy part. Getting the furniture to fit was tough. We can drop cloth it; we can bubble or blanket wrap it; but no guarantees. Oh, do people love their chair legs. One little scratch, and it was like you'd smacked their kids. And some jerk yells, 'That black man over there chipped my table,' when I know damn well he did it himself."

"But you didn't quit?" Leah was all ears.

"No, I kept at it. I remembered what you'd done for me. And one day I wanted to come here and tell a happy story."

"So, where are things now?"

"Not perfect, but much better. They promoted me to the warehouse. Let me keep a few books and records. An inventory guy. And now I'm a dispatcher, too. Keeping up with the guys on the road."

"William, I'm so proud of you. So very proud." Leah's eyes said it all.

"My wife's a receptionist for a hair stylist. Working to be one herself. The raises we got help us take care of our kid. She's going to be a real beauty, I'd say. Anyway, I'm never going to forget your help. Took a real chance on me. Laid yourself on the line."

William was genuine. So many failed second chances. But William's success and gratitude were real.

"Would you mind telling your husband my story? He seems like such a nice man. I never took the college-prep courses, but everyone loved him at the school."

Leah gave William a hug. "Keep it up and keep in touch. You're always welcome here."

Later that night, Leah said, "John, you should be so happy. Even kids who weren't your students think the world of you."

And, as she recounted William's story to John, for the first time in a long time, Leah felt worthwhile.

///

Leah was struggling to draft for a client a commercial real estate lease. She added this provision, took out that. Drat—nothing seemed to work.

"Why don't you run it by Jerry?" Mr. Hinkle suggested when she came by for help.

"Jerry? Please, Mr. Hinkle," said Leah. "I may be just Leah Richards, middle class, no special shakes, but still, I like to think of myself as a woman of taste."

"And so you are. But we're a small firm here, and can you imagine how Jerry feels with everyone freezing him out?"

With the guilt pack squarely on her back, Leah explained the situation to Jerry and asked if he'd take a look at the lease.

A while later, Jerry came back. He had drafted several provisions linking rent to performance that protected Leah's client without offending the building owner.

Leah managed, miraculously, to say "Thank you." What she thought but did not manage to say was "Not bad for a few hours' work."

The next day, the two parties came to terms.

"Well?" said Mr. Hinkle.

"I'm sorry, Mr. Hinkle," said his favorite young attorney. "This one still has a-ways to go."

13

A birthday present without a birthday. A Christmas present without a tree. Leah was pregnant.

John was gleeful. "Congratulations, Leah," he cheered, high-fiving his wife.

"Come now, I didn't exactly do this by myself."

No sooner did they start racing ahead with plans than Leah felt nauseous.

"It could only be one of two things," she fretted. "I'm either on the verge of a miscarriage, or the baby has some horrible birth defect."

"Nonsense. You're perfect, so how could your baby be anything less?"

"John, you're not funny."

"Sweetheart, you know, and I know, nausea is normal."

"Dr. John. Who would have guessed? You're going to have to do a double turn with dinner. I can't stand the sight of food."

///

Leah wanted to learn the baby's sex. John did not.

"For God's sake, John, not knowing the sex is so Grandma Moses. And I'm far beyond that."

"You are, and you aren't. You can't figure yourself out, and neither can anyone else. That's the glory of it. My intriguing, beguiling, ever-fascinating wife. But one thing we all know. What you need to do, you will do. That part of you the whole world knows very well."

"John, stop changing the subject. We're talking about the baby's sex."

"Then ask the baby. It's rude to talk about someone behind their back."

He made her laugh. "Darn if I don't believe you're going to win this one. I can't out-charm you."

"Well, you won't find anyone in Jane Austen asking about amniocentesis."

"Enough already, kiddo. I told you I give up."

So, they plowed through two sets of names, John enjoying the suspense.

And they prepared alternative baby rooms, festooned in blue or pink.

And the blue/pink baby shower, with Leah's friends wanting to know what kind of gifts to buy.

And they bought the balloons in two colors, and two of this and two of that.

"Don't worry," he assured her. "If you have boy/girl twins, we'll be well-prepared. And if we use all the pink for this one, we'll just save blue for the next."

"John, you're making this very complicated," she scolded. "We haven't even had one, and you're talking about another." But she was starting to have fun, enjoying her husband's creation of this happy drama.

///

The due date was in late April, sparing Leah the last trimester in summer heat. They talked about changes one night at Giovanni's, where the ever-joyful host had made a special meal as his own gift.

"This is what we've always wanted," Leah said, "but I'll miss the close of this stage in our lives. We were just starting to have fun again, together, and there's a part of me that's very selfish about that."

"Well," he said, "look at it this way. We're still young, and after we raise the kids, we'll have our senior years just you and me once more, that is if you'll still have me. By that time, too, our children will have become our best friends, and grandchildren will be our joy."

"Yes, but that depends on life being picture-perfect, and you never can tell."

"True, but if it isn't perfect, we'll still have one another to work through the problems."

At which point Giovanni appeared with delicious cannelloni, and the couple let the future fend for itself.

///

The baby was indeed born the image of perfection, a boy.

All the long discussions over names dissolved. They would call him Frank, after Leah's father, whom they both adored.

Visitors, too many of them, streamed in to see the newborn. "He looks like himself," Leah said after tiring of all the "looks like" comments. She felt helpless, not being able to chase well-meaning folks away.

A child at its best leaves parents in exhausted joy. They had never enjoyed sleep so much or had so little. John offered to get up at night, but since he wasn't breastfeeding, it fell mostly to Leah.

"Is it too soon to start playing Mozart? Yummy brain food, you know."

"Very funny, John. Not too early for Tolstoy, though."

Finally, they gave in and asked their mother's old caretaker, Mrs. Watson, for help. Ellen and Nancy would pitch in where they could.

John was holding his own as the only grown-up guy. The teacher in him came out with Frank, to Leah's delight. "Mozart aside," she said, "are you devising lesson plans?"

"Yes, and now it's time for recess to change the pupil's diapers."

"The great danger with first children is neurotic mothers," Nancy warned as John left the room to attend to the diapering.

"How I know," said Leah, remembering her own.

"And neglected husbands. Truth is, they always want you to believe they're neglected. When the kids were born, Jim acted like some older sibling, grabbing his share of attention in the nest."

"That's the way it is with women," laughed Leah. "There's only so much of us to go around."

///

They had to read up on babies, neither of them having been around too many. Dr. Spock and a million others competed for attention. Leah had no idea there were so many baby books. "No surprise," said John.

"Weddings and babies are billion-dollar industries." Most of the books counseled new parents not to panic or obsess. "So," John added, "you won't need to check on Frank every minute. Frank will join the conversation when he pleases."

It was a little soon for daycare, in their opinion, so Mrs. Watson became a godsend. Both Leah and John returned gradually to work, where their bosses proved understanding.

In a pinch, Leah was forced to rely on Jerry. "I'm sorry, Frank is running a fever," she said.

"Forget the Brunson letter. I'll take care of it."

What a shame, she thought, that someone that smart should be so odd. The most she could do was put him with a client on the phone, though even that was an improvement.

A judge? A jury? Forget it.

///

For a man who often smiled, Mr. Hinkle's grin this day was broader than usual.

"Mr. Hinkle," Leah stammered when she heard the news. "I've been on maternity leave. How can you want to make me a partner when I rush off at three to make sure Frank is all right?"

"Your colleagues love you. Your clients love you. You do more in a morning than others do in a day. And besides, you went to Harvard," he chuckled. "Think of the cachet."

John was planning a little celebratory dinner. The Hinkles would, of course, be invited, and the Fergusons, and Ellen, and after some discussion Henry and Katie, but Jerry?

"No, it's my dinner," said Leah, feeling her foot firmly planted.

"But he's been helpful to you."

"If you must know," said Leah, seeking an escape hatch, "it's Brigitte. It's like having a call girl at the table."

John was prepared to say no more.

"I'm sorry, sweetheart. You're planning this wonderful dinner for me, but you know how one person, just one, can spoil the whole shebang."

The dinner, when it came, was a grand success. The gamble on Katie's good behavior had paid off. And Henry, whom they feared might feel an outsider, had fit right in. Leah judged herself no sentimentalist. But the whole occasion, she thought, was a celebration of their marriage, their child, and the good folks in Woodson, a town that made life worth living and imparted the blessing of dear friends.

14

"John, I was just thinking, your parents have been out of our lives so long. They left our neighborhood many years back. But still, they live only ten miles away, and I almost never see them, except when I run into your mother at the grocery store. One day I did think I'd be adventurous. So, I made a Greek salad at the salad bar and brought it over to your mother. Artichokes and avocado and olives and feta. A great creation, or so I thought. Your mother just stared at it for what seemed the longest moment. Obviously didn't want it. Didn't bother to say 'no thank you.' Just barely nodded and walked away."

"That's not you, Leah. It's just her."

"But most people are thrilled to be grandparents. It's their first grandchild at that. You can't keep grandparents away. We've got to give it one more shot."

At Leah's urging, they made the trip. At the entrance to the new grandparents' driveway was a "No Trespassing" sign, as if anyone would ever dare. The gray stone of the house, the overgrown state of the yard—the whole scene radiated sequestration. "They make J. D. Salinger seem welcoming," John would say.

Leah knew she risked invading a patch of John's life that he preferred left undisturbed. His childhood had not by and large been a happy one. It wasn't just that her husband was an only child. His parents had all but left him to raise himself.

Finally, he spoke. "It's all true, Leah, and I can't entirely shake it. But as I've told you before, they played little part in my life. I might as well be a stranger on the street. The whole thing hurts me from time to time, and maybe it hurts them. They seem to live just for one another, and I feel I could live with their hostility more easily than I could with their indifference all these years. It's like two little icicles, up there on that hill."

"I hear you. But then again, with Frank maybe things can change. They're the only grandparents Frank will ever have."

So, they knocked on the door, this new family of three. The visit went neither poorly nor particularly well. John's mother did make tea, but his father uttered scarcely a word.

Leah's hope that Frank might help bond John with his parents faded fast. She thought it was a miracle that her husband had turned out as well as he had.

"Maybe he was upset we named our baby Frank," Leah said afterward.

"Whoever knows with him. But I did see him watching Frank on the floor, and I even thought I once saw him smile."

"Please come visit," Leah had said as they'd carried Frank back to the car.

"Do you think they will?"

"No. But stranger things have happened. At least we tried."

Leah was starting to think it might be better for Frank if they never tried again.

///

One afternoon, a truck pulled up to the Richards' residence. Workmen began spreading mulch over two perennial bare spots on the front lawn.

"I'm sorry, but there must be some mistake," Leah said when she spotted the activity. "It's a neighbor's house you're looking for."

"No, ma'am. Your husband called and wanted it. Said something about your birthday."

"What! I'll straighten this out with him all right when he gets home!"

"John," she sputtered, "what kind of practical joke is this?"

"No joke, Leah. The lawn has needed this for some time. And this is the best mulch money can buy. Chock full of beautiful wood chips, not just pine straw."

Leah rushed inside to grab a broom with which to swat her husband's butt. "John, this is my birthday, for God's sake!"

"And so it is," he laughed. "That's why I went for quality. Now I'll admit, mulch is never so beautiful as the first day it's laid down. So, as part of your present, we'll freshen it when the need arises.

"And frankly, I thought I was erring on the safe side, not giving you a year's supply of Windex."

"I should swat you, John, good and hard. It's my birthday! I guess I didn't really want that elegant evening out. Oh wait, I get it. So aromatic. This gorgeous, sumptuous mulch is, after all, Chanel in disguise."

And so, the couple spent an evening in what can only be described as delightful domestic discord.

"John, you are infuriating," Leah said, trying her best to sound serious.

Again, he drew her to him. "Watch out, sweetheart," he whispered. "High-end mulch will steal your heart in time."

///

"Birds hop. They never step," said Leah.

"We step. We seldom hop," rejoined John. "One way or another, we all seem to get to where it is we want to go."

It relaxed her, his habit of letting things be. On rare evenings, when all was quiet, the two of them returned to their old pastime of watching birds from the front porch. They watched the robins claim their kingdom on the ground. They watched the cardinals claim their kingdom in the bush. They watched the skittish towhees and the uptick tails of the wrens. They watched the magisterial blue jays with their magnificent black collars still try to hide their kinship with the crows.

They watched in blissful silence until Frank began to cry. It was John's turn to go in.

15

Suddenly, shockingly, the rumor reached Leah that John and Ellen had had an affair.

The rumor was detestable even by Gloria's standards. Leah knew her husband well; she would never believe it. Not with anyone. Never with her own sister!

But Gloria had done her sleuthing well. She had followed some scattered clues to Ellen's apartment, where she would hide behind a clump of bushes and watch John repeatedly go in.

In fact, Gloria congratulated herself on her stamina. Her whole life seemed to be building toward this moment. She willingly waited for hours to log the precise times John entered and departed the building. No ordinary person, Gloria thought, would have shown this sort of patience, but then this was indeed a once-in-a-lifetime opportunity, a chance to pay back John and Leah both for the way they used to snub her back at Woodson High. As a bonus, she could get Ellen too. She had never liked the Richards family.

The evidence she collected was too powerful to be denied. All that was left was for Gloria to fan the wildfire as Gloria alone could do.

"Please," begged Leah, desperation in her voice, "tell me this isn't true."

John sat silent.

"God," she screamed, "how could you!"

"Leah, it's been over long ago."

"Over! Why was there anything to be over with?"

"Sweetheart, Ellen was so shaken by the whole thing with Norman. I was so depressed by everything about Hank's death. For a moment there, we were all that offered one another any kindness."

"And you think I wasn't depressed by what happened to Ellen and Hank?"

"Leah, it was a hard time for me. And you've always wanted me to be something more than who I was."

"No pity party, John! No pity party. In case it didn't dawn on you, this tryst of yours was with my sister. My sister, John. My little sister!"

"Leah, please," the desperation in his voice now equaled that of hers. "We'll come through this. We've loved each other so long, and that has brought us through so much."

"There's been nothing—absolutely nothing—like this."

"Leah, please," he repeated. "We're happy together. More than anyone, you know we're meant to be. We have a gift from God in our beautiful Frank."

"John, I've lost my father. I've lost my mother. I've lost Hank. I've lost Ellen. And now you, John. You've taken yourself. I've lost you."

"Leah, I made a mistake. A horrible mistake. Please forgive."

But he wondered if she were listening any longer.

That night, as she began packing, she prayed for the wrath of thunder to wipe her from the earth.

///

John knew immediately he had made the mistake of his life. He beat himself up incessantly, so much so that the sin took sole possession of his mind.

He loved only her. He had committed his life to her alone. She got him. She understood the books he taught more than anyone he ever met. Without her, the characters lay dead on their pages. Without her, he had floundered in college. With her, he flourished in the job of his dreams. They say "one and only" is as much a fantasy as the figurines on the wedding cake. But he would forever believe she belonged, with the swirls and icing, atop that cake with him. Leah had given him her all, and in their difference, they found unity, as through the now-transgressed bounty of God's will.

John wondered where all this would leave Leah and Ellen. Ellen was nice, and she had a good, caring heart, but she was one-dimensional. Leah was many layers deep. Ellen had always existed in Leah's shadow. This would only add to the problem. He prayed that Leah might forgive Ellen, even if she could not bring herself to forgive him.

Little did or could he know how deep the fracture went.

///

Ellen sat on the end of a park bench whose gray boards, were there not splinters in the middle, would have accommodated three or four. A slight drizzle had settled on the park, but preoccupied minds take no heed of misty weather.

Lonely before the affair. Lonely and shamed after. She had made a mess of it. There was now little hope of a nice friendship with John. As for Leah, things were worse than a wreck beyond repair.

Normally quite put together, Ellen became suddenly aware that she had worn the same shirt three days in a row.

Who in Woodson would now look upon her kindly? She prayed silently to her parents, wherever they were, whatever they might find it in their hearts to do.

She had no family. No earthly family anyway. Still, she had to start somewhere. To find some connection. When she next came to the bench, she must remember to bring seeds. Maybe the sparrows would come and keep her company.

CHAPTER

16

Gloria had made certain that all of Woodson knew of the affair, which only added to Leah's humiliation. The thing was too juicy for the gossips to pass up. Wherever they gathered, Gloria was in demand. This time, they nodded, Gloria was on the side of truth.

Gloria, thought Leah. How did so angelic a name attach to so malevolent a being?

Leah had nowhere to hide. All the elders of Woodson clucked, "Tut, tut!" What business, Leah fumed, could it possibly be of theirs? Small towns glare down with a collective opprobrium, while large cities hardly seem to care.

"You seem scary furious," Nancy said to her friend.

She was. But the anger, she supposed, would fade with time. "The hurt is forever."

"You still love him?"

"I love the man I thought I knew."

She would miss Nancy's back patio. But Woodson, so long the source of fondest memory, had turned on her—her father's accident, her mother's stroke, her brother's drowning, her sister's perfidy, her husband's . . . she could hardly find the word for it, so she wiped away tears.

Nancy had never seen her friend like this. She had been so strong through so much. Now Leah struggled before her like a wounded bird, and Nancy wanted only to bind her wing.

"Is there any chance for the two of you?"

"No." The affair, to her, was incest, against all laws of God and nature, and who could ever put such a thing out of mind?

She was determined to go, and Nancy had learned long ago not to contest that incontestable will.

"I shall miss you, Leah." For many reasons, Nancy thought. Who would she now talk to, she wondered, as age began its slow advance?

"Oh, Nancy, I shall miss you too," Leah said to the person she would always trust.

///

The arrangements were hers to make. Given John's betrayal, he was ill-equipped to make an issue of anything, in or out of court.

She would, of course, take custody of Frank. Packing his tiny shoes gave her comfort, even as it saddened her with thoughts of all that might have been. John had bought Frank a little Penn State shirt. A bit young to be a Nittany Lion, Leah had thought, but then again, she knew how to humor men.

The business side of her took over. If only for a moment, practicality could stare down grief. She paid the real estate taxes, renewed the car insurance, and headed down to the bank to review her finances.

What to do with the house? She had purchased Ellen's share of the property their parents had left them. After much thought, she would let John remain there. Teachers earned far too little income, and if he would pay the utilities and see to basic upkeep and repairs, he could stay there rent-free. She had no desire to be punitive. It would hurt him and do nothing to heal her.

What about John and Frank? What had happened between the parents had nothing to do with their boy. She wanted Frank to have a father, even a flawed one, so she promised John she would manage somehow to get Frank to Woodson when he wanted to see his son.

She would see to a divorce in due course, but right now she had too much else on her mind.

She told Nancy she would leave a forwarding address first thing. But, truth be known, she had nowhere to go.

The one sure thing was to leave Woodson. Too many reminders of too much.

Mainly she was driving roundabout ways to avoid memories of John. Memories that were everywhere. Thornton's, where the milkshake club had met long ago. Giovanni's, where they had dined so many times and where she would leave a goodbye note. Woodson High, where his handsome face once seemed to her perfection.

She had to drive roundabout, else her tears would block the road.

///

Mr. Hinkle was crushed when Leah told him she was leaving. He was growing older, and he had wanted, in essence, to leave the firm to her. She was well-liked in and out of the office. Already, they were planning to make her a name partner.

"No need to explain, Leah," he said when she was trying to start. "I know."

He felt for the first time unable to give counsel. He had never felt before in her company the need to straighten his tie. He wondered whether women felt grief more deeply than men and whether he, were he faced with such a terrible situation, would try to make what he could of it, to reassemble the pieces, and somehow to muddle through.

He wanted to say a word about John, who was the favorite teacher of his niece at the high school. Alicia had said he was a kind and caring man, and his niece seldom misjudged people.

But he was silent. He sensed in her a pain so deep that to talk was to trivialize it.

Finally, after time slowed unbearably, he told her of a friend in Philadelphia, at Briggs, Abramstein, Roy, and Duckworth. They did white-collar defense and had a real estate practice. Would she like him to make a call?

Leah, still dazed and out of options, said yes.

"There are no goodbyes here, Leah. Only see you laters."

She nodded. Anything to avoid speaking. What he had meant to her was beyond the far reaches of her words.

She, in turn, had brightened his days in ways that only the spirit of youth can do. He saw sadness etch the pretty face he remembered and eyes whose only companions were her tears. She had closed the door behind her on her way out, which she almost never did.

17

"Mrs. Richards, I promise this will go without a hitch. By the way, that's a mighty good-looking lad you have with you."

William, Leah's friend and erstwhile client, was handling the move. The company would give her small collection of belongings top priority.

Leah had taken out a mortgage on a renovated row house in downtown Philadelphia, near where she worked. Cutting down on the commute would leave her more time with Frank.

As she left Woodson for Philadelphia, Frank was napping in his car seat, and Leah drove silent in her Ford. The Great Migration had hit towns like Woodson hard. Kids spent happy childhoods there, but the jobs and nightlife didn't hold them as adults. The towns they left seemed to mourn their absence; the faded signage alone seemed to speak of better days. Welcome to Woodson: Founded 1786. That sign had needed a paint job since her high school days.

Now she saw it in the rearview mirror as she headed into the woods and rolling hills just outside of town. She had not thought of becoming part of the town's exodus. She'd had a satisfying job, and Woodson was a far more vibrant town than most. But the mortification of it all and the shattered human glass in seemingly ever finer pieces left her only the road.

The drive started out somewhat easy, as the Pennsylvania Turnpike was a convenient artery connecting Central PA and Philadelphia. It left her alone with her thoughts. Or, rather, with questions. Was she foolish to let John into Ellen's marriage? To ask John to dissuade Ellen from marrying Norman? To want John to counsel Ellen during her horrific break-up? Was she too trusting? But then, what reason was there not to trust?

She went over her own marriage in her mind. Was she too hard on John? Had she taken his good qualities for granted? Had she locked him out too coldly after Hank's death? Was there some black hole between them she could or would not see?

Had she tried hard enough? What should she have done differently? And then, as the questions came so fast as to scorch her brain, a merciful moment of clarity emerged. Why was she to blame for her husband's betrayal? By what strange sequence should she turn upon herself? There was refuge in simplicity. This was John's fault; it was not hers.

But, as simplicity was only starting to take hold, her soft sobs woke Frank.

Frank, too, was crying now, so they stopped in Lancaster for lunch. The Amish buggies with their tired horses and outsized wheels still rattled down the streets. But there were fewer now, and Leah suspected many were for tourists. At night she dreamed of Philadelphia engulfing the entire state of Pennsylvania, and as its prosperous, high-tech suburbs spread ever west, the Old Order Amish and Mennonites prepared to wage their brave, final battle against time.

The turnpike deposited her about twenty miles outside of Philadelphia. She had to rely on the two-lane Schuylkill Expressway to bring her into the city. As she discovered that road's notorious traffic, which had earned the hatred of all Philadelphians, her thoughts seemed to start and stop with the bumper-to-bumper vehicles. She arrived at the townhouse, tired in mind and body. The last lap between the city's outskirts and its downtown had seemed endless. William did what he could to cheer things up. "If you'll open these blinds, you'll get some nice morning sun."

"How's your daughter, William?"

"Her teacher says she'll make her parents mighty proud."

He left, and the night in all its loneliness descended. No one to share the childcare and household duties with.

"That's okay, Frank," his mother said to the sleeping boy. "We'll make a go of it, we will."

///

At the Briggs law firm, Leah felt she was starting over. She came in as a salaried partner—highly paid, but with a higher cost of living, too.

Other differences would also take some getting used to. Eighty-odd attorneys was not large for a Philadelphia firm, but just this one modest firm was bigger than the entire legal population of Woodson. Her office was on the seventh floor of a twenty-two-story building, and its small window looked out onto other tall, glassy structures. If the inhabitants of a city feel somewhat hemmed in, such is the price the city pays for having a prestigious skyline.

What to do with the office walls? Hanging her law school diploma and bar admission certificate would mark her as professional but also fungible. She thought of a French Impressionist print, but that, too, had come to seem conventional. She settled, finally, on several abstract paintings. They were pleasing on their own terms, and most importantly, they did not remind her of anyone or anything.

Late evenings those first days in Philadelphia were the worst. The loneliness of a large city at night swallowed her whole. Leah tried to take stock. She and John were now a thing of the past. They would, as in college, go their separate ways. Separate lives lay before them. Although he was only about two hours away, impassable distance lay between them. Regaining trust was a journey of ten thousand miles.

She needed to take her mind off it. She turned on the television. Many channels, none of interest. She opened a magazine to read with an aimless late-night snack of cookies and milk. She flipped through catalogs in search of something she might actually want. All blah. Suddenly, she shook herself back into purposefulness. Leah Richards. That name meant something. That she knew.

No matter what, she was a survivor. Whatever she had to do, she could and would. Matchless grit and persistence her mother in her best days had taught her. Divorce, betrayal, desertion, death, and widowhood. Every woman, Margaret Richards warned, would sooner or later be thrown upon herself. The thing was to dig deep, deep and survive, survive. Face it down, whatever "it" happened to be. Survive! But survive for what? And for whom? Her father taught her the sweetness of companionship. His namesake might one day bring his gentleness again into her life. Survival only drained the softness from existence. It was the coldest of comforts. Survival, even if one managed it, was an arid way to live.

But it was what she had to do. Endless to-do lists. Check off this and that. Take more off the list than you add on. Keep the grocery and the cleaning lists separate. Leave her keys and glasses by all means in one place. Meet this client and that colleague and this caretaker, and manage to smother the pain in your heart. Miss at unsuspecting moments the one man with whom it had become impossible to ever reconcile. But make it through. Somehow. Survive.

///

The days were mercifully busy. The Briggs firm did some work for the Philadelphia Flyers of the National Hockey League, and when one of the lawyers on that team left unexpectedly, Leah was thrown in. Much of the Flyers' work was done in-house or by league lawyers, but there were contracts everywhere—transportation and lodging on the road, concessionaires, uniform requisitions, trademark and licensing agreements, and the like that the Flyers wanted their specialists from Briggs to review. Personal injury suits arose from time to time, and the lawyers even became consultants on media relations and the legal ramifications of sexual assault and substance abuse. There were the occasional interactions with the players and their agents, but Leah, as a professional sports neophyte from Woodson, was not overwhelmed by proximity to stardom as it seemed a few other lawyers in the office were.

Mr. Roy was the senior partner assigned to make Leah feel welcome, and Alex, the lawyer two doors down, extended a helping hand as well. "I spend all my time with scoundrels," Alex complained, but not too loudly because white-collar defense could be profitable stuff.

"Scam artists, money launderers, swindlers, bilking the elderly at every turn, then lying to me, their lawyer, just as they'd lie through their teeth to their own mother if it meant an extra dime."

Leah knew the problem. "They don't play straight with you. It's really hard to convince a jury of their innocence if you can't even convince yourself."

"Mr. Roy was supposedly assigned to me," Leah mentioned one day to Alex, "but since I've got here, he hasn't spoken a word."

"It's not you," Alex said. "He's just an all-around cold fish. Chilly Roy, we call him at the firm, always behind his back of course. But then he's got a real beat on the local insurance practice, so he's welcome."

Of course, Leah thought. A big game hunter lionized in Philadelphia. In Woodson, a drip.

///

Katie, by now a CPA in Woodson, had weighed in with a typical Katie comment. "I can't believe how much you must be making now," she wrote. "It makes me drool just to think about it. God, what I'd give to be pulling down your figures."

Same old Katie, Leah thought. She was the first in the class to open a lemonade stand, and she just loved being around rich people. Leah was pleased for Katie that she had a job close to money.

It was not that Leah turned down her nose at those who made money, or that she didn't enjoy making it herself. Money intrigued her, so much so that she attended some lectures on the subject at Harvard. The lecturer talked about the different forms money took—equities, fixed income instruments, negotiable instruments of all sorts, and the different ways various societies treated credit and debt. But the most fascinating discussion involved ancient coins and the profiles of Roman emperors and British kings and queens who adorned them.

"So, you can see from these coins," he'd said, as he passed them around the classroom in their protective casings, "how much money has meant to countries, indeed how all of civilization is constructed upon it. You may think the invention of fire or the adoption of laws was a greater leap for humankind, but I am here to tell you that money surpasses them all. These coins didn't just massage the egos of rulers. They let the ancients value one another in ways that didn't involve the winners of brute combat. They united countries through a common currency. Nay, more than that, they lubricated commerce and freed us all from primitive bartered goods and transactions. So, if you think I worship money, you are right. The noble purposes of money overwhelm the evils of greed and corruption."

Reading Katie's letter and recalling the lectures, Leah reached in her pocketbook for some coins and sifted them slowly in her hand. There were Jefferson nickels and FDR dimes, some shiny and bright and others worn with use and age. Money was a simple thing for her, which the lecturer had missed in all his high-falutin' words. She wanted money for her family, for parents who now would never reach old age, for Frank's brothers and sisters who now would never be born, and, most of all, for John, so he could live the life he wanted and teach forever.

18

There was less and less time for thought. Frank was almost three now, and Leah had found a good day care, or so it appeared. Frank seemed happy to arrive each morning and happy at the end of each day. It's a young child's face, not a parent-teacher conference, that gives the best report.

Leah found two neighbors with children at the center, and they were able to share carpooling and arrange play times during the weekends and later in the afternoon.

Then one day Frank fell off a slide and had to be rushed to the hospital, where his cut lip required several stitches.

He would be just fine, but the whole thing unnerved Leah.

"I'm sorry, Mrs. Richards," explained the supervisor. "We just can't keep track of everyone every minute."

"But isn't that why we leave our kids here—for you to do exactly that?"

"Mrs. Richards, I promise. This will not happen again."

Everyone makes mistakes, she thought. On balance, the center seemed a good place, one that didn't just warehouse children but tried to stimulate and engage them.

The whole routine, however, was exhausting her. Her practice required meeting client demands and racking up billable hours.

When Frank got sick, she had to break from work, pick him up, and (hopefully) leave him with a neighbor.

Home at day's end was playtime with Frank until he finally dropped off to sleep, whereupon she paid bills, emptied trash, sorted laundry, and played catch-up on the legal work she couldn't finish in her stop-and-go day.

If she went out for an evening, she called and called for a sitter, some of whom worked out, others who did not.

"Why not come home to Woodson?" Nancy asked when she sensed the fatigue in Leah's voice over the phone.

"The practice is really stimulating here, and Frank and I are slowly making friends. But mainly, there's so much past in Woodson, it would take two lifetimes to work through."

"But you won't know unless you try."

"I can't face it now. Just tired of being tired. All I can do is work things day-to-day."

///

Things could always get worse. Leah noticed the pipes had sprung a leak, which she figured out from the soft, bulging baseboards.

She needed a dry wall man to rip out the wall, a plumber to spot and patch the leak, the dry waller again to replace the wall, the painter to repaint it. She inquired furiously around the firm about whom she could rely on.

"Mr. Roberts, is ten a.m. Thursday the only time you have? It's my son's doctor's appointment."

The other end of the phone was non-responsive.

"So maybe I should call in several days to see if something opens up."

"Probably best." Next call, Leah thought, she should feign a male voice.

The plumber, when he finally came, forgot to bring the right equipment. "Be back in half an hour." Another morning wasted. Such a seller's market. Leah, not long on patience to begin with, was going crazy.

///

Back at the office, three of those dreaded pink call-back slips to tie up the afternoon.

At the end of the corridor, Leah heard a voice berating a young lawyer. The door had not been closed, and the voice rose without a hint of letting up.

"How do you expect anyone to like this crap?"

"Mr. Green, I've worked hard and—"

"It doesn't show it. All it does show is that you're the most pathetic attorney, if you deserve such a title, that I've worked with in twenty years."

Leah hurried down the corridor. "Mr. Green, no one can work with you raving on. And Sandy is not your dog."

"You've been here three months, young lady. Who exactly do you think you are?"

"That question is one you'd best ask yourself," Leah retorted, shocked at hearing herself doubling down.

Just then Alex stepped in. "She's right. Of course, all of the young lawyers need criticism, and all of them need to work weekends, if necessary, but my God, Philip, it's your tone. People are fleeing you like the plague."

"And just what do you plan to do about it, Alex?"

"What I plan to do is go to the executive committee and have Sandy transferred to a boss who treats him right."

"I should have handled it more diplomatically," Leah said to Alex afterward.

"Not really. We've tried diplomacy for years to no effect."

Alex followed through and Sandy was transferred. "He's doing capable work, as best I can tell," said Alex, "and no one is complaining about his effort or temperament."

Leah knew Mr. Green harbored deep resentments.

But there were no more raised voices down the hall.

///

The city quickened its pace, but Alex at least was providing a reprieve. He was a native Philadelphian, and Leah liked the way he could negotiate the city. She admired his savoir faire and was amused at the fuss that waiters and store clerks made over him. It was this elegance of service Alex attracted, without seeming effort or request, that Leah enjoyed on their outings. Also, he was single. The two of them had taken the summer associates to lunch, and then to dinner, and finally decided to try a dinner themselves.

The restaurant was perfect. Alex had chosen a trendy spot along Rittenhouse Square, the city's most popular neighborhood for well-to-do young people. And he had reserved an outdoor table with an excellent view of the park in the middle of the square. Whether in summer garb or festooned with Christmas lights, its trees imparted an undeniable romantic air.

"I knew you'd be the authority on the wine list," Leah laughed as he selected a bottle of Beaux Freres Pinot Noir. "My friend the wine snob."

"I bet you find it expressive."

"Whatever is that supposed to mean?"

"Sip slowly and find out."

"Alex, I have a question. Actually, a serious question."

"Okay."

"What makes a successful big-city lawyer?"

"Working hard and loving luck."

"But how does one love luck?"

"Well," he said, "they call her Lady Luck for a reason. Hug her next time she's at your door. She'll befriend you ever after."

"Oh, is that it?" she laughed, easing into flirtation.

No more earnest questions for the evening. No shop talk to spoil the fun. Alex had a gift for lightening things up. In a crazy way, she thought, he might also just be right.

He took her to a Flyers game and explained, patiently enough for a guy, off-sides and icing, the role of the front line and defenders, the penalty box, and the power play until Leah thought herself capable of bluffing through a five-minute conversation on the sport.

"Thank you so much, Alex," she said as he dropped her off at the end of an evening. "You've made me feel so very welcome here."

///

Making sure John saw lots of Frank was another challenge. The arrangement Leah settled on was, as they say, unusual.

She would drive Frank down to Woodson on Friday, where William or Nancy would pick him up at a Subway restaurant just outside of town.

Or, if John wished, he could drive to Philadelphia and collect Frank at a neighbor's down the street.

Leah was proud of her ingenuity. John would get to see Frank the whole weekend, while Frank's parents would avoid the awkwardness of meeting face-to-face.

Everyone besides Leah thought the whole thing weird. And even Leah was beginning to resent the fact her foremost companion was a car.

"If you don't mind my saying, Mrs. Richards, because it's really none of my business, but it wouldn't turn the world upside down if you laid eyes on your husband."

"William, I can't tell you how much I appreciate your help. I admit the whole thing is convoluted, but it just makes it easier this way."

"Maybe, but I have to say that little boy is mighty happy with his father. They do neat things together, outdoors if possible. Frank being cooped up in the city all week, your husband takes him to parks to run up and down, zip around on his scooter, watch the birds, and learn the trees. They're even planning a field trip to Gettysburg."

"How do you know all this, William?"

"Frank and my little girl are becoming great friends."

"Really," she smiled.

"Yes, and Frank and I are becoming buddies, too."

///

Alex was pushing Leah faster than she was ready to go. Recent friendships for her were like saplings that needed time to grow.

She certainly was not ready for physical intimacy. But, then again, she understood that most men had one foot on the accelerator, and it was unfair to blame them completely for their innate need for speed.

There were so few women partners at the firm that women had no choice but to befriend men. And besides, she liked Alex. She never felt like she was interrupting him. She could drop into his office anytime.

How could anyone not like Alex? He was smooth, as well informed as he was well connected, a quick study whose personal and professional skills made for a great future at the firm.

And he was not all about himself, his conversation not boorishly served up with "I," "me," and "my."

"How about this entrapment defense?" Alex was preparing for trial. Knowing her criminal defense background, he would run things by her.

"I don't think those fly," Leah cautioned. "Trying to convince a jury that a police officer persuaded a criminal to commit a crime won't hack it. Better save it for sentencing. Absence of criminal disposition. A judge might buy that."

He was fun to talk law with. In fact, fun generally. "How about a little canoeing this Saturday?" he said.

It had been years since Hank's death. Leah had slowly, haltingly, recovered her love for streams and rivers, but she wanted to bring Frank.

"I'd love to do that, but maybe next time. Frank's a great kid, but it's extra special, just you and me."

Leah relented, and Alex planned the excursion. Once on the water, she felt free. "Whoa, Alex, whoa!" she laughed and shouted as if on a roller coaster. He paddled straight for white water; the greater the challenge, the quicker the thrill. The spray refreshed her face; the sun and breeze left Philadelphia far behind. When Leah climbed finally from the canoe, exhausted, she made Alex promise to bring her soon again.

That evening, Leah felt a little guilty. She had missed a weekend afternoon with Frank. She worried she had treated Hank's memory too casually. And Alex's mastery of the moment had made him devilishly attractive. This last thought gave her pause, but not for long. The two of them had had a grand old time.

CHAPTER

19

At times the law of gravity can be a blessing, pulling people back to fondest sights and sounds. Other times it is a curse, blocking departures and grounding dreams.

No matter how hard Leah tried, Woodson would not let go. If only one could leave past and place behind by snipping strings. How much lighter we would be. Or so Leah mused one day as she supposed a nearby flying bird to be carefree.

A small envelope lay on her table. She had no need to open it. She knew what was within.

Katie told her on a visit to Philadelphia that Ellen was engaged to be married. A fellow realtor. They had been friendly competitors. They would now join forces.

It was, thankfully, to be a smallish affair. Leah knew that Nancy would want her to come.

"After all, she's still your sister."

That's the point, Leah thought. She was.

"If I came, Nancy, it would be like nothing had happened. But it has."

"The favor of a reply is requested," read the card.

Coming to the wedding meant dredging up the past. Leah checked the Regrets box, nothing more, and dropped the card in the mail.

///

The sad news came from Woodson that Mrs. Watson had died. She was in her early sixties, not old, but beset by heart problems that had worsened considerably over time.

This time, Leah would go. Mrs. Watson had been there when the family needed her. With her mother in her last months and with Frank in his first. She shared with John the belief that last caregivers were often forgotten but always should be given their due.

The funeral was at the graveside, and John, as expected, was in the small gathering. Their heads bowed, there was no need to cast glances at each other.

Leah was not sure whether her grief was for dear Mrs. Watson or for all that had happened to her and John.

She ran into him as she left. She had prepared for the possibility. "Thank you," she said, "for your kindness to Mother after her stroke."

"I hope you're doing well, Leah," he said.

After the funeral, they had gone their separate ways. It was as she anticipated. The anger had subsided, but the pain had stayed.

It wasn't until she arrived back in Philadelphia that she had time to take it all in. She caught a deep breath, tossed an indifferent dinner in the microwave, and thought about the slightly drab but lastingly precious quality of dependability that Mrs. Watson had come to represent. Someone comforting even out of your presence because you instinctively knew where they were and what they were doing. They hadn't talked a lot, Leah and Mrs. Watson, because they hadn't really needed to. She thought, as she tidied up for the evening, that perhaps at this moment, it was just possible that John missed Mrs. Watson too.

///

The announcement arrived with great fanfare. Hank Richards would be posthumously inducted into the Woodson High School Sports Hall of Fame.

This was Woodson's grand accolade. It was a greater honor even than the Chamber of Commerce citizenship awards. Hank had become, Leah thought, one of those remarkable people who resonated far beyond the grave.

The whole family would be expected to be at the ceremony.

Leah asked Jim and Nancy to arrive with her, as the occasion promised to be one of tearful meaning and awkward greetings. The auditorium was a large one, too cavernous, Leah feared, for the event about to unfold. But the crowd swelled shortly to a size where, if the need arose, Leah could get adroitly lost.

The stage itself seemed pumped for the event. The dignitaries were primed. The last-minute microphone testing gave the whole affair an air of due importance.

"This evening we honor one of Woodson's finest," the principal intoned. "One whose own life was risked continually for the lives of others. One whose love of country knew no bounds. One whose devotion to friends and family inspires us to this hour. One whose like shall not soon pass Woodson's way again."

Coach Ramsey followed, which caused Leah to squirm uncomfortably. "On the field, he was all spirit," he recalled for the audience. "In life, as in football, he was knocked down, but always up again. On one leg, he was unbowed. In football season he shone, but he was truly a man for all seasons and for all future generations at Woodson High."

Katie was next, and she read from transcripts of interviews with Hank's classmates and teammates. Highlight film from Hank's high school games was shown. Hank's retired jersey and number were unveiled.

The family sat in the front row. Leah and John sat on either side of the Fergusons. Ellen's new husband sat between her and Leah. It was left to the Fergusons to keep the conversation, what there was of it, going, and the entire row had been relieved when the program began and silence (and cell phone turn-offs) was requested.

For Leah, what might have been a happy remembrance seemed immensely sad. It brought back to her, and undoubtedly to John, the tragic circumstances of Hank's death. Almost as bad was the seating. The Richards family, once so happily close-knit, sat hearing of their brother so awkwardly apart.

///

Leah's plan for Frank's weekend transfers had mercifully collapsed, its silliness apparent to everyone involved. Now she would drop Frank off directly at John's on many Friday evenings and pick him up there Sunday afternoons. John would sometimes come directly to Leah's to get Frank in Philadelphia.

Even Leah was glad to see the old arrangement go. Frank was growing older now, and Leah and John didn't wish him to see the strain. They now spoke amicably, as many separated parents do, for the benefit of their child.

They were both proud of him. He was proving a bright, happy kid whose teachers predicted great things. "One thing we agree on," John would say. "He has great genes."

One Sunday, John proposed they take Frank to the Philadelphia Zoo. He was sure that Frank would love the giraffes. To his parents' surprise, he also took to the reptile house and aviary. He was what bound them now, and it had been a good afternoon.

"Is there any chance for us, Leah?" John said as he prepared to leave for Woodson.

"Oh . . ." Leah said, caught off guard in the moment, despite the delightful effect of the outing. "I don't think so. I'm exhausted half the time. But I like my practice here, and we're settling down and making friends. Mainly, honestly though, I just don't think I can ever get past it. I don't think it could ever be the same."

CHAPTER
20

Alex had bought a place on the Cape. Cape May, that is. This quaint New Jersey town had supplied wealthy Philadelphians with Victorian-era shore houses since the mid-1800s. The place was, as they say, a bit of a reach for Alex, but with his job and the prospect of appreciation and some rental income, he got a sweet mortgage with only five percent down.

His Victorian beach house promised a host of new connections. Important, interesting friends. And it enabled easy conversations with the senior partners at his firm, who owned similar houses. The one downside was that the venerable homes felt a bit antiquated—a natural state for houses built in the 1860s and '70s. That was no matter for Alex, however. He hired a leading interior designer from Philadelphia to modernize his mansion. No period furniture. No old, stuffy feel. Instead, his home's interior had a sleek, modern design. Contemporary art. Expensive furniture. A fancy wet bar and modern wine cellar.

Summer was his season, August his month. The area's restaurants never failed to please with their Cape May salt oysters, lobster tails, and lengthy wine lists. After dinner, a walk on the beach. It was comfortable to walk barefoot because the city government used heavy machinery to smooth the sand every night during the summer.

Late afternoon cocktails on the porch with pals. He had worked hard, and Leah did not begrudge him his ambitions or his dreams.

He wanted her with him. At least for a week. Alex was fun, and she wanted to go. Frank would love the beach. Maybe find some friends.

"You wouldn't want to leave him with your husband?"

No, she thought. Having Frank along would slow things down. August could be hot in more ways than one.

"Jeez," he exclaimed when she mentioned separate bedrooms. "I'm being punished for things I didn't do."

Leah, uncomfortable, tried to explain, but Alex said no need, apologizing for jumping too far ahead of where she was. She wasn't ready; he didn't need to understand it, he said, and instead he encouraged her to bring the little fella for the trip.

Alex was a good sport about it all. He played with Frank in the water and made him grilled cheese sandwiches for lunch. He waited quietly while Leah put him to bed.

"You've been very patient, Alex," she said one night after Frank was asleep. "I know you're wondering is this girl of yours a deep freeze. All I can say is I've been through something very traumatic that caused my body to lock up. I know this has been hard on you."

"Well, I won't pretend it has been easy. Not when you care."

He sat still, as if summoning the nerve for a next question. "Do you think you'll get divorced from your husband? You've been separated for some time."

"Probably. Eventually. I don't know. We go way back. It's just going to take some time."

Alex went in to grab a good-night glass of wine. He returned to the porch with his turtleneck on.

"I'm sorry to unload all of my complications on you, Alex. It's so nice being with you. The air and water and your company have been good for me. Things will sort themselves out before long."

21

Walking downtown one day, Leah bumped into an old acquaintance—at least she thought he was.

"Jerry?"

"Leah!"

"Jerry, I hardly recognized you." He had trimmed down, dressed sharply, and looked to all appearances like the proverbial Philadelphia lawyer.

"What are you up to?" she asked.

He had, regrettably, left the Hinkle firm. "You and Mr. Hinkle were the only ones really nice to me. Got quite a few cold shoulders."

"I didn't feel I was very nice to you, Jerry, but I'm pleased you thought so. Anyway, I'm anxious to make amends."

"I heard you were with the Briggs firm. Doing work for the Flyers."

"Exactly right."

"I'm only two blocks down from you. At Cordell. On the corporate transactions team. Mergers, acquisitions, take-overs, even a public offering or two."

"That sounds like a lot of territory."

"Seems pretty specialized to me. But I wanted a challenging practice, and that's what I've got."

"And Brigitte? How's she?"

"Sad to say, we're divorced. She wanted Bohemian. I wanted respectable. Actually, that's overstating it. I wanted to stop shoving my disreputability into everyone's face. I'm engaged though. Helen has a son from a previous marriage."

"Wow! How do you feel about that? If you don't mind me asking."

"Honestly, I'm not sure. Have no idea what it's like to be a stepfather. Whether I'd be any good at it or not."

They stopped a moment for some coffee. Jerry's decaf habit hadn't changed.

"I don't at all know how Tim's going to take to it. He's six, and it must be rough on a kid to have two fathers. Some days I wonder whether Roger, that's his natural father, and I will be in some competition for his affection."

"It must be rough on you, too, Jerry. Being in the house with some-one else's son. Some nights, when Tim acts up, you must just want to utter some unutterables."

"The whole thing's uncharted territory, that's for sure. But I love Helen deeply, and we're going to try to make a go of it. By the way, Leah, I was so sorry to hear about you and John. You might one day be wondering about Frank the way Helen is about Tim."

"Actually, I'm wondering now. I like this guy at work a lot, but I don't know how it would go with him and Frank."

"No way to tell. Marriage is enough of a leap without something like that."

The office now beckoned them both. Jerry picked up the tab, and they promised to have lunch. Leah mulled the surprise encounter all afternoon.

22

Ellen and her new husband, Marty, set up Rainbow Realtors as their agency. They groused the way realtors tend to do at weekend work and fastidious clients.

"Those people looked at sixteen homes," Ellen complained. "Still not satisfied. I told them it might be best if they got a new realtor."

"The sellers can be as bad as the buyers," Marty replied. "The Carters still wonder why their house isn't moving. Well, guess what? They priced it ridiculously high; it needed repairs; it was not even in clean condition, and the Carters are not especially friendly people."

Mostly, however, the agency did well. Both Ellen and Marty were outgoing, and they knew not just houses but people. Ellen did still suffer the occasional hurt. A prospective seller volunteered one day that she would never want an agent "who fornicated with her brother-in-law."

Mainly, Ellen was hurt that Leah had not come to her wedding. She and Marty did not plan on having children, and, other than her husband, Leah was the only member of her family left. She composed a letter in her mind for months, finalizing it only after numerous false starts:

> *Dear Leah:*
>
> *I can never properly express how sorry I am for what I did. I must apologize a thousand times over for what must have hurt you a thousand times. I can say only that the great share of the fault belongs with me, not John. I am especially sorry because you have never been anything but kind and protective of me after Mom and*

*Dad and Hank died, and after Norman's abuse. You deserved so
much better. Again, I am sorry, and I love you.*

> *Your sister, always,*
> *Ellen*

Leah read the letter several times. She worried that correspondence
with Ellen would eventually lead to the two of them meeting face to face.
She could handle almost anything, but she could not handle that. She
would never wish Ellen ill, but the only way to get past it all was to put
her sister out of mind. Any guilt was Ellen's to deal with. As for herself,
she desperately did not want to resurrect again and again something she
wished so fervently to leave behind. Why wouldn't Ellen at least accord
her the small decency of leaving her in peace?

> *Dear Ellen:*
>
> *Thank you for your letter. You were nice to write. You know I
> shall always wish you well. And if you are ever in extremis, I shall
> always be the first to help you out.*
>
> *Absent that, for your peace of mind and certainly for mine, I
> do not wish to refresh the memory of it all, but just to let it rest.
> So please, with only expressions of best wishes, let this bring our
> correspondence to a close. It will be better for us all. I do thank you
> so much for your understanding.*
>
> *My best,*
> *Leah*

///

Leah was poring over a licensing agreement when a cheerful young
woman came up.

"You must be Leah Richards," she said.

"Yes, I am, but pardon me, do I know you?"

"In a way you do. I'd heard you were here. Your brother saved my
life. I'm J—"

"Baby Jenny!" Leah leaped up and gave her a big hug.

"Well, not exactly," she laughed. "Jenny will do."

Jenny had come with an invitation. She and Deandra, her significant other, would like her for dinner next Wednesday night.

When Leah arrived, she found a striking contemporary apartment with abstract originals from Philadelphia's most promising painters and brown-and-blue-themed area rugs, chairs, lamps, and tables.

"I know people would love a Matisse or Picasso," Deandra explained, "but even a quality reproduction is way beyond our means. Besides, we want to give the good locals a shot. Of course, Jenny's tastes are oh so Western."

"Western!" Jenny jumped in. "Who wanted the picture of the sunset over the Acropolis?"

"There you go, Jen. Getting modern on me again."

Leah found herself enjoying the sparky banter. Their love of life was contagious. The evening was spent catching up, or rather getting acquainted, since they had never really laid eyes on one another before.

Jenny had gone to Cornell undergrad and was back home in her second year of medical school at Temple. She hoped to become an ER doctor. "I know the malpractice premiums will probably be sky-high, but emergency rooms are the front lines and, frankly, I owe my life to someone who responded to an emergency and saved me."

Jenny thought the medical profession would prove welcoming. "Really, what folks want is a good doc, and they'll respect the personal choices."

Deandra was majoring in drama at Penn in hopes of one day becoming a director. "It's a lot to learn," she admitted. "Sets, costuming, lighting, audio, and how they all fit. And whew! The stage has more than its share of prima donnas, and managing all those big egos is going to test my patience to the absolute limit. I've learned that even from the student productions."

They were happy to share each other's plans, and though they were young, they seemed to be aware of the problems any relationship brings and the hard blows life inevitably lands. But they had come out together, told supportive families at the same time, and even their most conservative friends had wished them only the best. "I don't know that your courage merits a gift, but if it doesn't, it should," one conservative friend told them. Knowing Deandra's interest in the theatre, he'd gotten them tickets to her favorite Broadway show.

"Being a lesbian does have its amusing moments," Deandra offered while they were on the topic. "Really good-looking guys. They ask you out. Think they're God's gift to whatever, so irresistible that they're bound to flip me. But I am who I am." The three women drifted into conversation about the local arts scene, Philadelphia up-and-comers, and other such chatter as the night wound to a close.

The whole evening struck Leah as quite perfect, another little piece of evidence that Hank's brief life was not in vain. She and Frank were indeed making friends and settling in. He was enrolled now in Springside Chestnut Hill Academy, a fine private school in northwest Philadelphia. The school stressed its college preparatory curriculum. "I hope not for Frank," laughed Leah. "He's only in first grade."

23

Then came news that Leah refused to believe. Alex was being investigated for embezzlement.

She didn't want to discuss it with anyone at the firm.

The amounts involved were apparently substantial. As much as half a million dollars.

Worse was to come. Not only was Alex suspected of taking money from the firm, where he now served on the executive committee and was unofficial treasurer, but he was thought to be in league with several accountants on the firm's payroll.

To top it all off, he may have diverted funds, which were held in trust for clients, to his personal account.

Leah was stunned. It was too much to take in. "Remember," read the memo from the managing partner, "Alex has denied any wrongdoing. He is entitled to a presumption of innocence as the investigation proceeds."

Leah was too flabbergasted to talk with Alex. Who to turn to? She was scheduled to have lunch with Jerry the next day.

"How does something like this happen?" she asked him. "I mean, Alex was a guy with the world in his hands. If anyone had a future, it was him. No way that this makes sense to me. That he would put it all at risk."

"You're right. It's not rational."

"Then why? Why!"

"Consider it this way," Jerry said. "Embezzlers most often start out with small amounts. They persuade themselves they're only taking out a loan, that they'll repay it when they get the chance. And then they get away with it. So, they move on gradually to larger and larger sums. And then, too, they're often overextended financially. Or in debt."

Leah thought of Alex's Victorian mansion in Cape May.

"But," Jerry continued, "extravagant or not, it becomes an addiction."

"Yes, but how can they think they wouldn't eventually get caught?"

"Often they don't think about it. Or they get some sort of thrill playing the odds. In Alex's case, maybe he learned every trick of the trade defending those shysters. Perhaps he thought he could do them one better. Anyway, I have no idea what was going through his mind. It's all speculation."

Leah hoped it was all some big mistake but feared it was not.

Alex's counsel called her the next day and asked if she would be available as a character witness. Not knowing the facts, she said she would not.

In three weeks, an indictment came down. As if awakened from a dream, she and Alex were over.

///

After the episode with Alex, Leah lost faith in herself. She wondered if she would always misread men. No man, she thought, was ever what he seemed.

Maybe the sexes were ultimately unknowable to one another. Maybe men were just unknowable to her.

Then she thought of her father and Mr. Hinkle. But to her now, they seemed almost alone in pristine goodness, the exceptions that proved the rule.

At such moments, Mr. Hinkle always urged her to take a walk in a park. It was the solitude that cleansed her mind, and she was being thrown more and more upon herself. Solitude was not loneliness, she thought, and the formations of rock and design of leaves had their own consoling powers. The coneflowers warmed to the sun, their lavender petals drooping mournfully from their orange-brown thistle cores. Such sadly postured things of beauty, Leah thought, as her mood embraced their blooms.

But then, nature at the end only let her rationalize her sadness because nature, sooner or later, reminded her of happier times and more carefree days. And those invariably were spent with family and close friends, whose number now dwindled before her very eyes. Family, once gone, does not return, and friendship, like those old oaks around her, takes years to grow.

She sought out a bench. Maybe Frank, when he was grown, would become her best friend. He already was, in a way. Sometimes, when she watched him make up childish games, she wished more than anything that he might have had a brother or sister, and she and John a larger family. But like so many things, John's liaison with her sister had cut that short too.

An old man wandered by. He seemed smart but shabby, all at the same time. Harmless. Leah sized him up quickly.

As he did her. "You're too beautiful to be sad," he said. "If I were young once more, I'd want to be Prince Charming and sweep you off your feet."

Leah could not suppress a slight smile. The years of homelessness had taken their toll, but he hadn't lost whatever spark he'd carried before his misfortunes. Passing time in idle talk was probably what he did best.

"Songs," he continued. "They romanticize us. Hobos, drifters, ramblers. Don't believe it. I've spent a life on the road, running away from I don't know what.

"Pardon my French," he said, "but being homeless sucks. Some fellas ply their trades on favorite street corners. Dangerous to close in on their turf. Bad weather, shelters tend to get full. Soup kitchen to soup kitchen, I've had 'em run out. I, myself, am what they call a nod head. A lifetime of opioids. Less and less of a high. More and more needed to drift off. Even my best clothes belong in a dumpster.

"Well, I didn't mean to go on. Like I said, you're too pretty to be sad. All I can tell you is I wish I had your life."

With that, he wandered off. Leah thought a moment. This man knew nothing about her. He was crazy to think she had no problems. Did he know what deeply personal loss was like? Different problems, but hers were no less real. Of that she was sure. But poor guy. What a raw, hard life. She did not know what to make of it all. The old man had shared a kind moment with the sad countenance of a stranger.

And he had a point.

John had continued to live in the Richards family home. He and his old Woodson High classmate Henry would occasionally head out to dinner together, with Henry's wife half-joking that she desperately needed a husband break.

The two of them had a comfortable friendship, their conversation drifting to whatever happened to come up. Henry was not, as they tactfully say, "a student," but he had an eye for opportunity, which had led to community college and an electrical contractor's license.

"I don't try to oversell homeowners on fancy burglar alarms," he told John. "Better they have a dog with a bark that keeps Philly awake."

Henry's specialty was flood lights, and his clients were mostly small businesses. "They're vulnerable because they're unoccupied at night. Woodson's growing, real slow to be sure, but the growth brings business and, sad to say, business brings crime."

"Glad at least we grew up in a town of unlocked doors," John said. "I don't suppose there'll ever be a town like that again."

Henry said he'd had some friends visiting him last weekend who stayed at the Comfort Lodge. "And darned if the assistant manager on duty wasn't Gloria. She went out of her way to help my friends and said she'd been working there about four years."

"Funny, I didn't think Gloria could hold a job that long."

"Me neither," said Henry. "But when I asked Gloria if she had heard of some classmates, she just seemed to clam up. Maybe because there were so many guests milling around in the lobby. Maybe because she hadn't kept up with anyone. Maybe because it's all something she's just trying to forget."

"Who knows?" said John. "Gloria's always going to be Gloria. I doubt she'll ever change, and someone that mean isn't worth trying to figure out. Anyway, back to business for a moment, I need your help in bringing more light into the Richards house. I think Leah would want that. A home can be bright and lively with a family, but with just a solitary occupant, it suddenly seems so dark."

///

To the Fergusons, John was the best kind of neighbor—the quiet kind. He had a good sense of humor even on a Monday, but Nancy observed he brightened considerably on weekends, when Frank, and sometimes Leah, would come into town.

Katie was nice enough to put Leah up for the evenings. Sometimes they got along merrily; other times, not so much. It was one of those friendships where many years of spats and hugs promised many more.

"Let's take him to Gettysburg," John proposed to Leah one spring Saturday. Frank was a third-grader now, old enough to understand the history of the place.

The number of statues and monuments befuddled Frank, but he was not at all in doubt when John took him to Cemetery Ridge to help repel Pickett's charge. A plaque marked the "high water mark" of the Confederacy, the spot where the 72nd Pennsylvania Infantry drove back Pickett's assault. "Boom!" John shouted. "Reload, Frank, reload!

"Boom! Look at all those Rebels coming at us over that big field, Frank. Watch your cannon ripping holes in Rebel ranks. Boom! You did it, Frank! You did it! You beat them back."

After the tide was turned and the battle won, Leah led John and Frank to the spot of Lincoln's Gettysburg Address. It was short enough to read to him.

"You see, Frank, all those people defending that ridge back there fought and died for something very important—that we remain one country, whose citizens, black and white, will be forever free."

"That was beautiful," John said.

"I was a little worried that Frank might imbibe too much of the battlefield atmosphere."

"Not a chance. That little guy is way too studious to be a warrior."

"Wonder why. A literary father who's also a historian. Lucky guy."

As they drove back to Woodson, the weary warrior was napping in the back seat. "Would you like to stay over, Leah?" John asked.

"I'd like to, but Frank has his friend's birthday party, and I've really got to take advantage of a mother's break to catch up on some work. Maybe some other time. Thanks to the two of you, though, for such a special afternoon."

///

So, Leah was off once more to Philadelphia, leaving John the bare limbs of a lonely week ahead. He was not accustomed to feeling sorry for himself, but he did wonder how the cost for a long-past mistake remained so irreversibly high. The frustration of not being able to say anything or to do anything that would give him a second chance was slowly taking its toll. He was neat by nature, but his dress and housekeeping were becoming slovenly by degrees. How could she not detect a loneliness that left so many clues? She opened life to him. Her absence left him imprisoned in his thoughts, as dank and dark, he felt, as any cell.

At Woodson High, John continued with what had been a labor of love. But he was growing stale. He needed a change. He was not the teacher he once was. It was a bit more of a duty now, and he needed Leah to discuss the books with him at night. Still, he changed what he taught each semester to try to keep himself fresh.

He tried *Oliver Twist* because he could throw himself into the story of a young boy on his own and because Sikes' brutal treatment of Nancy might alert his class to the evils of domestic abuse. Still, he wondered if Leah would have drawn something from the novel that he did not.

Some nights, the Fergusons invited him for dinner. Some nights, he dined out with different friends. On others, he cooked at home. When Leah left, he thought he might at least take the opportunity to become a gourmet chef, but it wasn't much fun cooking just for oneself.

His desire for companionship was intense. Louise, a single chemistry teacher at Woodson, had long been his friend. They went out to dinner on occasion, and John was grateful to her for breaking the loneliness that often awaited at the end of his day.

Louise admired his judgment. And John was widely commended around school as someone who put students first. For a literary guy, he was also practical, and he had developed a knack for simply getting things done. Even when she knew he was low, he would do his best to raise her spirits. His decency and their friendship were for real, and Louise had hopes for something more.

Louise was talking at dinner about chemistry lab that morning, and the dread of chemistry teachers everywhere—that some inattentive student might do something dangerously dumb.

She noticed he was not listening, that his eyes and mind were far off.

"John, you're not present."

"Excuse me, Louise. I'm sorry."

"You still miss her, don't you?"

"Yes, I still do."

She tapped his hand and decided to herself, Okay·then, we'll just be friends. It wasn't what she had hoped, but it would be enough.

///

Nancy, by her own admission, was a small-town gal. "Every time I come to Philadelphia I want to get out of here. Too much traffic. Foul air."

"Oh, come on, Nancy," Leah reprimanded over dinner. "You're always selling the city short. This is where our country really began. And the Big Five. They're always bringing in speakers and performers. So much to do here. If," she sighed, "one only had the time."

"Leah, you've been brainwashed!" Nancy laughed. "You need to get back to your roots."

"I hear you, Nancy. But before you leave, go by the Franklin Institute. There's more there than you could absorb in a lifetime."

The truth was Leah was learning to negotiate Philadelphia herself. Not just knowing which risky neighborhoods to avoid and which traffic bottlenecks to skirt. She became acquainted with the grocery stores, restaurants, dry cleaners, and post offices in the area, and she'd made friends up and down the street. Small neighborhoods within large ones within cities within regions within the state—concentric circles in which many city dwellers learn to create a sense of community, even intimacy. But to Nancy, it was all just one big urban blot, so Leah kept the thought to herself.

The friends lingered long into the evening. "I'm sixty-two now," Nancy said. "My joints are starting to act up on me. Gardeners are benders. Can't work in the yard the way I used to. Our bodies are funny, aren't they? How can the same thing dish out so much pleasure and so much pain?"

Nancy began filling Leah in on the latest from Woodson. "Your friend Katie is always asking for my recipes." The thought of Katie annoying Nancy to no end made Leah laugh out loud.

Nancy tossed tidbits here and there. "Ellen and—"

Leah interrupted. "Let that one be. Case closed."

"Understood. But, at the risk of unsettling you, John misses you so. Jim and I really like him as a neighbor. To be honest, our fondest hope is to see you two reunited. We keep thinking, two such good people. Why are they apart?"

Leah was indeed unsettled, but she had reached the point where she could talk about it with her friend.

"Nancy, Frank and I are making a life in Philadelphia. He loves his school. The practice here is stimulating."

"There's something you're not telling me."

"You're right." Leah hesitated. "If I moved back, I don't know how it would go with John. Whether we could recapture what we had. Whether I even want to, after everything. I just don't know."

"Well, you could give it a chance."

"I will say this. He's been a wonderful father. None better. Frank loves his dad."

"Couldn't he still be a wonderful husband too?"

Leah began fiddling with her fork. The conversation was becoming difficult.

"Nancy, think if this had happened to you. That's what makes it hard. All the good folks offering advice. It never happened to them! The affair lasted several months at least. Maybe longer. I don't even want to know."

"Leah, I would never in a million years want to excuse what happened. But it's also quite a while ago."

"It is and it isn't. There are times at night when I can't get back to sleep. I set my life on that man. I would have done anything for him. And then he did the one thing that most nearly destroyed me. It's been a long road back. And there's miles to go."

"I know, darling. I can't even imagine living through something like that. But maybe, just maybe, it would now help your own healing to forgive."

"We'll see. But must forgiveness mean I also trust? I'm just not sure I ever could. Anyways, I've never had any desire to punish him. I'll only wish him well for as long as I live."

"I know that, Leah. But doesn't faith teach us to forgive?"

"It does. But what happened here violated every religious principle I've ever known."

This time it was Nancy whose eyes filled with tears and Leah's turn to console. "Oh, Nancy, I've never had a dearer friend. It can't be forced. But things are better now between us. They really are."

What Leah anticipated as an ordinary lunch involved an extraordinary proposal.

"First, the good news," said Jerry. "Helen's pregnant."

"Wonderful, Jerry! Do you know yet: boy or girl?"

"A girl! Tim's little sister. Four months away. Helen and I have been so happy together, and this just makes it all the sweeter."

"I should say." Leah looked over at his face. It was a nice moment, entering fully into the joy of a friend.

"Anyway," said Jerry, "the prospect of parenting two kids set us both thinking. Helen thinks Philly might be a bit of a rough place to raise kids. And besides, private schools and a big home and yard to run around in are all way beyond our means, especially if we have another one."

"That makes sense. Living here's not cheap." Leah had no idea where all this was headed.

"So, oddly enough, I started thinking once more of Woodson."

Leah was stunned. "I thought Woodson was the place you couldn't wait to get away from."

"Quite so. But that was the circumstances. I wasn't really welcomed at the Hinkle firm, nor should I have been, given my contrarian persona. And Brigitte and I seemed to be arguing every night, while Helen and I, we just talk things through."

The more he talked, the more sense Jerry seemed to make. Woodson wasn't a perfect place by any means, but it was still relatively free of drugs and gangs, and it had a group of citizens intent on keeping it that way. A decent public school system and still, for the time being at least, a good place to raise children.

Then came the whopper. "So, Leah, I'd like for you and me to start our own small law firm. Richards and Yates. I'm not naïve about the effort it would take. But just to be out from under big city billable hours, and answerable to ourselves, at least to some extent . . . well, what do you think?"

"Wait." Leah was about to fall backward. But Jerry had paid her a compliment and she was not about to reject it out of hand. "Jerry, really, you've taken my breath away. There's only a million or so things I need to consider."

"Think of it this way, Leah. We've always worked well together. Even when you weren't sure of me—and I know you weren't. But we've come around and we've both succeeded. And between us, we've practiced in a lot of different areas. And Mr. Hinkle is set to retire in a month, so we wouldn't be competing with him. We could even ask him to come on Of Counsel."

"And to think I thought I was just sitting down to enjoy a midday hamburger with you."

"I didn't mean to take away your appetite, Leah. Here, I'll order another so you'll get the chance to finish yours." He chuckled, flagging down the waiter.

///

Leah emerged from her luncheon with Jerry able to think of little else. Returning to Woodson had been the last thing on her mind. She would visit, of course, but she had given up on actually living there for good. Turning the pages of a book is all in one direction. Life, she supposed, was much the same way.

For a moment, Leah thought the whole thing hopelessly impractical. Too ridiculous to even waste time thinking about. Frank was happy at SCH and doing well. She continued to like her work with the Flyers. Besides, moving was a huge pain, and she didn't even know where she would live.

But Philadelphia was becoming almost unmanageable. Motherhood increasingly meant carting Frank here and there. The hours in all big-city law firms were long, and she spent much of her day in a state of near exhaustion. Woodson at least offered more ease of movement, and if starting a firm was a major undertaking, it might prove a refreshing challenge, too. She didn't relish the thought of competing against her old firm, but without Mr. Hinkle, it was not at all the same place.

And Jerry? Could the two of them work well together? Increasingly, she thought the answer might be yes. They lunched regularly, and their discussions showed the kind of intuitive and unspoken understandings that mark the best professional partnerships. His mind was something else, and Leah still had enough old Woodson connections to bring in some business.

Putting Frank in public school? The schools still had college-prep tracks, and it might do Frank some good to know more kids from different backgrounds. If it didn't work out, there was a decent private school three miles outside of town to try.

Then, of course, lastly but most importantly, John. Things had reached an equilibrium between them; not all great, but not an altogether bad situation either. The pain had lodged geologic layers deep in their relationship, and to go to Woodson might force the issue, bring it all to the surface once again.

A thought sometimes invaded her mind of which she was ashamed, but which she was not always able to repel. She and John were apart so much, and as the saying goes, separated men feel free to roam. She did not think he would, but how could she be sure? The doubt was small, but it was there. Once upon a time, there would have been no question. But did trust, once broken, become something impossible to wholly restore? And could she even blame him at this point? She'd gone out with Alex, and she and John had led their different lives for so long. She was surprised at how strongly she still did not want him seeing someone else. Even now.

Her friends, most of them anyway, had wondered why she hadn't chucked the relationship, sought a divorce, and moved on long ago. After all, he had crushed her core. Delores, a friend she had met and liked in Philadelphia, had filed for divorce on the basis of much milder transgressions. "It's something no woman should ever have to put up with. We have to put the guys on notice," she declared.

Nancy, almost alone, persisted in urging forgiveness. "He's a good, good man. Men like that don't come along every day. And Frank needs a full-time father."

"Leave off," Leah said. Nancy often made rational but not visceral sense. She had not experienced it. She had no idea how it felt to be betrayed.

"I still love him, Nancy," Leah added. "But I can never and will never forgive what he did."

"Forgiveness is whole," her friend replied. "You forgive the whole person. Right now, you're splitting him in two."

But Nancy let go for the time being. She was glad her friend had come as far as she had.

Splitting in two! Leah could not forget the words. People sometimes thought her so put together when her whole life she had actually been split in two. Her father's pride/her mother's worry. Harvard Leah/Woodson Leah. Big-city Leah/small-town Leah. Professional Leah/maternal Leah. Married Leah/separated Leah.

She was alone and weeping now, deep into her pillow. "I'm so tired of not knowing who I am," she sobbed, thankful there was no one to hear. She could not resolve herself; she feared she would die unsolved. So many women, she screamed within herself, were flung into this purgatory of non-identity. So many men seemed to know not just what they wanted, but when and why.

"Leah," John had whispered to her years ago, "stop fighting yourself like some gray bird at the side mirror of a car." As she recalled the words a muffled sound came from her pillow. The one man who might make her whole had split her more in two.

26

"To be, or not to be." That was Hamlet. But it was, John thought, in an odd sense, Leah too. The matter was dragging on and on, trickle by trickle, and Leah's conflicted mind seemed to him no more made-up than that of Shakespeare's immortal character. No resolve to live together. No divorce to keep them apart. At best, half-reconciled. A friendly faceoff. But then again, no anger to bleed their wounds anew. Leah made Hamlet downright resolute. How was he to force the issue? He loved her too much to ever leave her, not as long as there was hope. She would always be beautiful in his eyes. He had never met anyone as deep, as strong, as enterprising, as giving—at least before he scarred her for life. No one else had or would come close. Of course, he knew that any healing would take time. But days stretched into weeks and into months and into years. How sad that the girl who rescued him from childhood loneliness became the woman who sent him back to solitude. Not that he could fault that woman. But, if she would not act, he must. Their lives were not forever, as in the timeless song of Willie Nelson, "Funny How Time Slips Away."

///

Leah and Frank were traveling down to Woodson for the weekend. After much deliberation, she thought she should make John aware of Jerry's proposal. He might even help her make up her mind.

When they got to the house, however, they missed the familiar signs of John's presence. The lawn had not been cut. There was no air of welcome.

Just then, William drove up.

"Hi there, Frank," he said.

"Hi, Mr. Smith."

William explained he had helped with the move.

"What move?"

"John has moved to Allentown."

Leah's confusion was growing by the second. "I mean, why? What's this all about? He didn't say a thing!"

"I think maybe he'd best explain it. Here, he wanted me to give you all his contact information—new phone number, street address, and so on."

"Well, that's mighty decent of him." Leah was as peeved now as she was perplexed.

"Come on, Frank. We're going to get to the bottom of this." They were heading to Allentown.

"What's Allentown like, Mom?"

"Honestly, Frank, I have little idea. The only thing I remember is a Billy Joel song by that name, which laments cities in decline."

"Is Allentown in decline?"

"No, that may be Bethlehem. Knock it off, Frank, you're distracting me. My mind's on other things."

///

Leah had no idea that Allentown would be this big. In fact, she marveled that her home state of Pennsylvania was so big and that she knew so little of it. A college friend had mentioned only that the Lehigh River Valley was reinventing itself, looking to education, healthcare, and cleaner manufacturing to replace the departing steel plants. It was good, her friend had said, but also a bit sad, because Bethlehem Steel had been, like Popeye and spinach, the flex of America's industrial might.

Her friends in Philadelphia, however, often thought of northeast Pennsylvania as unendearing, if they thought of it at all. Allentown was no Philadelphia by a long shot, but Leah suddenly realized it had enough of a skyline to be imposing. It seemed to her that the whole city was under construction, one big development project. Leah noted the Lehigh River, some nice and not-so-nice neighborhoods, and a medley of decay and revival that made her think the city had seen better days but was also bouncing back from the bottom. The parks, playing fields, museums, and civic center were fine as far as they went, and the distance from Philadelphia and even Woodson was not impossible, but none of this began to answer the question: What in heaven's name was John doing in this place?

They pulled up at a small frame house that did, indeed, show signs of welcome, and John bearhugged Frank as he ushered them in. Leah observed once again how men living by themselves can make-do, can establish functionality more easily than personality. The furniture could have belonged to anyone. Still, the house was passably neat and, of interest to Frank, had a basketball hoop in the driveway.

"Why don't you go out and shoot a few?" Leah suggested.

"Can Dad come with me?"

"No, Dad's going to sit right here."

"Well," John said, "it's not as if I didn't expect the fifth degree."

"John, what gives? What on earth are you doing here?"

"It's a long story, but I'll make it short."

"No need to make it short, John. Just complete."

"I thought Allentown would present a great opportunity to bring literature to disadvantaged kids. So great, in fact, that I'm back in middle school, though they've promised me the first high school opening."

"Fine, but that's not complete. There are disadvantaged kids in Woodson too."

"Well, life in Woodson had been closing in on me. That's the only way I know how to put it."

"How do you mean 'closing in'?"

"I mean I couldn't escape my past. Incredible as it seems, there are people still blaming me for Hank's death. And others won't have anything to do with me because of the terrible mistake Ellen and I made."

"John, you're strong enough to deal with those things. You have for a long time."

"Just so you know, and to put all cards on the table, my friend Louise, whom you've met, and I had lunch with Ellen and her husband before I left. I simply wanted to wish them well."

Leah was shocked. Past was becoming present once again. "You told Ellen before you told me?"

"I had to tell a number of people. At the school, where I was resigning my position. And a few friends around town."

"Fine. Okay. So, your wife, which I still am, was at the end of the line?"

"Leah, you would only have tried to talk me out of it. And you're the one person who conceivably could. So, I had to tell you after it was a done deal. I was determined to go."

"Easier to ask forgiveness than permission. Is that it? John, we've never resolved things that way. Through avoidance."

"Nor would we resolve them that way if we were together. But we're not."

So much to process. Why did John not cut Ellen off cold? Why were they so much as friends? Shunning anyone was not his nature, but it hurt; he should have known.

There was more to come. "Leah, you asked me why I've left Woodson. All I've given you figured into it. But you're too astute not to know the biggest reason of all."

She sensed she should stay silent. The sparse furniture turned even more still.

"Leah, you were present in Woodson, except that you weren't. You were everywhere. I came back home every night to a house where you and I once lived. Ate at tables by myself where we once ate together. Slept alone where your warmth was once beside me. Left the house for a town where we grew up. Worked at a school we once attended. Taught books all day that we had discussed long into the evening."

"Please, John, honey," the last an inadvertence. Frank could come back inside at any moment, and he deserved to see his mother composed.

Quickly, to stem the flow of his remembrances, she filled him in on Jerry's proposal.

"Are you going to accept?"

"I really don't know. I waver back and forth. Philadelphia, for all its excitement, is a bit of a grind. But often I wondered, what would coming back to Woodson mean for you and me. Can we still get back something of what we had?"

Just then Frank appeared, wanting John to play HORSE. Both parents straightened themselves at the sight of their son.

"Dad, watch out, I've been sinking five straight."

"I'm no slouch myself, son."

Leah pulled back the curtains, tame white little curtains not meant to obscure a view of the outside. She watched from the window as Frank took his father to the cleaners. He was growing up fast. This time, she could tell, his father had not let him win.

She had rolled it over and over in her mind and decided, finally, to tell Jerry yes. Her attachment to the Briggs firm had faded after Alex had imploded. And after exploring to the last detail the whole idea with Jerry, she began to warm to it. This just might work.

How odd that this person she once found so repellent had become her best professional friend. It was as if the rain had come to like the sun. She came to enjoy his new wife, Helen, and Frank and Tim were becoming pals.

In the back of her mind was the thought that, with her there, John might one day return to Woodson. Maybe. She was not sure how exactly that would go, or even how she wished to proceed, but Frank was wanting to see more and more of his dad.

Anyway, that was all in the future, and with the present crowded, Leah put the tomorrows aside.

She and Jerry made plans to rent a small set of offices with room to expand if things went well. They would hire an office manager and two associates. The practice would be a general one. Their backgrounds covered the waterfront—criminal defense work, commercial real estate, contract negotiation, and transactional work, especially for small businesses. Leah even liked intellectual property problems, and who knew when one might arise. They were inclined to take much of what came in the door.

Mr. Hinkle had retired, but out of loyalty to his old firm, had declined any formal association with their new one. Still, he was both pleased and amused that they were together in Woodson, and he was not above offering avuncular advice.

"It takes years to develop a name and reputation, so don't be discouraged if things aren't going great guns at first. Also, the bars in these small towns are very close-knit, so don't be surprised if they don't take kindly to new entrants."

"I do have friends in other firms," Leah reminded him.

"Yes, you do, but this is business. It wouldn't shock me if they didn't refer you much, at least at first."

There was no way they could meet the overhead without a loan.

"I fear there's an oversupply of lawyers in Woodson." The loan officer at Woodson Commerce and Trust was becoming more skeptical.

Finally, Leah pledged her home as collateral. There was no other way to get the funds.

"I'm sorry," Leah apologized to her house as she entered it that evening. She and Frank would live there, now that John was in Allentown.

"You've seen a lot of me, old home. As a baby, a teen, a newlywed, with Hank and Ellen, then John alone, and now me again. Treat me kindly, old homestead. I'll do the same."

Nancy was delighted to see Leah and Frank back. "It's still Jim and me next door," she said.

///

Mr. Hinkle had been right. Things were slow. Their new associates, Jill and Juan, were eager, but there was not that much for them to do. Jerry had styled himself quite the "football coach" for his efforts to recruit Juan from Penn to a small Woodson firm, and he worried that Juan might soon regret his choice.

Other things were proving choppy too. Frank missed his friends from SCH. He was a fifth-grader at this point, and he asked if some of them could come and visit. "On your birthday maybe," Leah said.

Leah, for her part, was decompressing. Part of Woodson was familiar, part of it was strange. It was larger than the town she left. Good for business, perhaps; different from the days when things were settled with a handshake.

Despite its growth to a less-familiar modest suburb, Leah was having trouble settling into Woodson's slower rhythm compared to the City of Brotherly Love. Philadelphia had hyped her more than she supposed. Such different places, she mused. She recalled scouring a map one downcast evening for an area more exciting than Woodson, less driven than Philly. Alas, every dot on the map had problems of its own.

She and Jerry had long talks. Reality had caught up with their dreams. They wanted newer furniture for the office to impress clients, but there was no money for that. They talked of letting Jill and Juan go. Through no fault of their own, they were billing much less than their salaries.

"I don't want to do that to them," Jerry said. "It would be a horrible first professional experience."

A last resort, Leah agreed. They remembered their own early years.

The two of them planned to get out and around town more. To go to town hall and school board meetings. To join a couple of civic clubs. Jerry had wanted to be a Rotarian anyway. To go to local and state bar meetings. In short, to hustle; to make their own luck; to not sit back and expect anything from anyone.

"Some days, you just can't catch a break," Jerry said. "And then, suddenly, you do."

///

"Jill, you are about to become a domestic relations specialist."

"Really, ma'am. I never expected anything like that."

"Try it out. See if it fits." A friend of Leah's in Philadelphia was seeking a divorce. Would Leah be willing to represent her?

Not the ideal line of work, Leah thought. But in the circumstances, she said yes.

"You see, Jill, the economics are like this. The Philadelphia lawyers are expensive. Their clients are often in extremis, and the attorneys sometimes take them for a ride. We can offer real sympathy and better rates, by far."

"Will we be representing the husband or the wife?"

"We'll be representing men, dear. It often works better that way in court, the lawyer the opposite sex from the client."

"I hate to get in the middle of someone's marital breakdown," Jill confessed. "I wonder whether, as a lawyer, it's appropriate to feel sorry for both sides."

Leah was finding the conversation painful. "This one should be less difficult, Jill. No children. Besides, there's good to be done. Sometimes, through no one's fault, things just don't work. We'll try to release couples from their misery with a minimum of bitterness.

"If, that is," she added wistfully, "getting a divorce is really what they want after all."

///

John and William had kept in touch. William had risen through the ranks to become vice-president of the moving company. He had snappy business cards, and his name now appeared on the letterhead. The Richards had given a lot of business to Quicker, Safer through the years. William just wished he could move them all to the same town.

"Your husband has been good enough to tell me about your new firm," William related to Leah. "And how you and your partner are cracker-jack attorneys. He suggested we give you a shot at some of our legal work. We have more than we can ever do in-house."

Leah was always glad to see William, but never more so than now. Old friends, she thought, sometimes arrive with new ribbons. A moving company, Leah and Jerry were quick to grasp, promised a bonanza of legal business.

There were employment and human resources issues; regrettable roadside accidents; damaged furniture, real or alleged; potential disputes over trademarks or with the manufacturers that made all those different-sized vans.

"So, we'll start things off," William promised, "and I'm sure my bosses at Quicker, Safer will love you."

William would never forget what Leah had done for him. It no longer needed to be said. He knew she and John had been through a lot. Sometimes, he thought, when you get to know people apart, you wonder why they're not together. Well, it was none of his business. Whatever he could do for them, he would.

Leah and John were now staying at each other's houses on weekends, though not in the same bedroom. Frank was just beginning to feel part of a family; he could sense the thaw.

They were enjoying one another again. The trips to Allentown and Woodson were for themselves, not only their child.

"Stop it, John, you're making me laugh." It got to the point where he could jolly her up again.

"Snap to, John. Can't you see I'm talking to you?"

"Me see." He was impersonating Calvin Coolidge. Silent Cal.

"John, I said I was talking to *you*."

"Who you?"

"I'm Leah."

"Me Cal."

"Speak up, Cal."

"Up."

Whereupon she pounded and pummeled him until the Quiet Man was forced to issue his last loquacious utterance: "*Fini*."

"Really, Leah, it can't be as bad as all that," he would say when she donned her gravest face.

He could tell what was serious and when Leah was just getting revved.

"Okay, I give up. If you're not going to take me seriously, I don't know why I should even waste my time telling you all this."

"Because you know I'm interested. Help me with the title of that Shakespeare play. *Much Ado About* . . . Help me, Leah."

"All right, my little court jester." She engaged in the surrender of a laugh out loud.

John went to the refrigerator to check out their dinner. "Yep, it's here," he said of the salmon. "So often I'm reduced to takeout or some last-minute pick-up. Don't know why I can't keep a well-stocked fridge. Do you have that problem?"

"John, you know perfectly well that on this we're polar opposites," she said, smiling at her use of polar. "In my fridge, there are always items that have overstayed their welcome. The new arrivals have a tough time being squeezed and fitted in. I actually got a new freezer to solve the problem, but there's never enough room."

Leah took a deep breath. "John, all this time I've been spending in the car has got me thinking. You and I have seen so many early deaths, people taken from us far too soon. Mom and Dad, I miss them every single day. Hank and even our old classmate Chip. Such harsh consequences for one brash act. Our dear Mrs. Watson. A kinder spirit I've never known. She too died way too soon.

"So, I keep asking the question everyone must at some point ask. How could God, if God exists, possibly let this happen?"

"Of course I ask the same thing," John said. "Maybe we just can't expect God to correct things He can't possibly be aware of. But that answer doesn't satisfy me, so how could it help you?"

"Is it fair to assign a gender to God?" Leah asked.

"No," he replied. "It's just a shorthand."

"Do you believe in God, John?"

"Let's put it this way," he said. "That we're here on earth seems a question for science. Why we're here seems more a matter of faith. But the two are bound together by human curiosity, and I'm encouraged that so many famous scientists believe in some sort of divinity."

Leah was struck once again by her husband's depth. "And you, John. Do you believe?"

"Leah, the night sky is much purer over Woodson than in Philadelphia, or even Allentown. And I look up at the stars in all their majesty and see the hand of a creator."

"Not just some vast, impersonal cosmos?"

"Maybe not a total paradox. Not knowing anything, for sure, though, I try to ask myself what I should do. It all goes back to what Mr. Hinkle told us some years back. Just be kind to one another. If there is a God, and I believe there is, He would approve."

At that he was quiet, but Leah knew he might add something more.

"All the great religions of the world are trying to figure out these questions, Leah, and you should talk to theologians who know much more than I do."

"I would never discuss these things with anyone but you," she said.

///

John had moved up to high school lit once again. He was becoming as popular a teacher in Allentown as he had been at Woodson.

Something else, however, was also exciting him. He was for the first time teaching adults. "Literature in Your Life" his course was called, and it was part of a continuing education program offered in town.

Leah decided to slip unnoticed into one of his lectures.

"Remember," John was saying, "literature is chiefly for enjoyment, not instruction. It's just the pleasure and interest that comes from reading how others live life."

Those in the room were attentive. John was no local celebrity; that was not his nature. But he was developing a following because he touched his audiences with truth.

"Still there are times," he continued, "when literature does teach in a way no other medium can.

"Let me tell you a little story. I once had two students, I won't tell you their real names, but let's just call them Bill and Sally, and they were paired together in an essay competition.

"'I can't stand Sally, no one can,' Bill complained as he approached me after class.

"'Oh, I don't know, Sally seems pretty and bright to me. Here, take this home and read it. It's called *The Adventures of Tom Sawyer*.'

"The next day Bill came to class whistling about his good fortune in being paired with Sally. Pretty soon, when the other boys sensed he was serious, they wanted to be paired with Sally, too. She was no longer an outcast, which indeed she never should have been.

"Well, it all went back to the day Tom Sawyer whitewashed Aunt Polly's fence. If you don't like something or someone, try to pretend you really do, just like Tom did. You may change your own mind, and even if you don't, you may have others green with envy."

Leah loved the turn of his mind. She hadn't quite thought of things that way before.

"You really live literature, John. You absolutely do," she told him at the conclusion of the lecture.

"These great classics are out there, Leah. These absolute treasures, just waiting to be read. But it's sad in a way. Every day, there are thousands upon thousands dying who have never read *King Lear*."

"Oh my gosh!" she exclaimed. "How did you ever fall in love with a Learless girl? I'll make amends tomorrow."

///

"It's still nothing like Giovanni's," Leah said. She and John had discovered a nice Italian place in Allentown, but what could compare to their favorite restaurant?

"John, I really wanted to thank you and William for sending the Quicker, Safer business our way."

"I was only too happy to help. But it was really William's doing. How's that going, by the way? You seemed pretty discouraged a while back."

"I was and still am. But things are picking up. Slowly, I must say."

"Leah, maybe there's something we should discuss."

With that kind of an intro, Leah was apprehensive.

"Is it possible for you and Ellen to at least begin speaking again? I mean, there's this deep cut running right down the middle of the family. Maybe it would be a bit easier for us if we could put it in the past. Maybe when I'm next in Woodson, you and I could have dinner with Ellen and her husband. And we could ask Jim and Nancy or the Hinkles if you'd like."

"No, John, it's a non-starter. On that one thing, I've always been clear. You and I are starting to put some pieces back together. Seeing her, let alone sharing a meal like we're all chums, shatters everything all over again."

"Okay, but maybe there's a time to remember Ellen as the person she was to you—your sister."

She held his hand. "There's a time for some things, honey. But, for me, never that."

///

When she was bone tired, Leah would drift over to Nancy's once again.

"Nancy," she said one day, "all these years, you and Jim so happily married. What's your secret?"

"I suspect it's the thermostat. Winter, 68 degrees."

"Ultra-compatibility, I'm sure. Anything else?"

"Jim and I have our frothy moments. But really, we don't mind listening to each other's complaints over and over. His patients always complain. The dental hygienists are always sick. The suppliers always raising prices."

"Doesn't that get to you?"

"He's had a long day. Who else is he going to complain to? What about you?"

"Well, I always had a new case. John a new book. So, we kept it lively."

"Past tense?"

Leah just smiled.

If some sediment had settled on her neighbors' marriage, Leah thought, the reassurance of familiarity was not always a bad thing. "Jim's fixing lots of teeth. Taking patients out of pain. I've got a good man there. Good men, your John, my Jim."

Leah started. Nancy could do that to you.

"Come back early and often," her friend said. "Always happy to bring out the Woodson in you."

29

Things were slowly improving at Richards and Yates. Jerry was proving a good partner who more than upheld his end of the deal. Clients found he had their back. And his family loved Woodson. Jerry had taken up fly fishing, and he would bring Leah pictures of himself, all booted up, casting for trout across a frisky stream.

Quicker, Safer had become a good anchor client, and Leah was representing several associations that were resisting the construction of a shopping center undesirably close to some of Woodson's oldest and most beautiful residential neighborhoods. She determined to fight the developer on the proverbial beaches and hedgerows over this one.

Nationally branded stores and many other attractive boutique outlets were in the works. Teams of attorneys from Philadelphia descended upon the planning commission, zoning board, and supervisors to get the approvals they needed. The neighborhoods couldn't afford the high-priced lawyers, but the one they did hire went at it with a pitchfork, and the public swarmed every meeting.

"I know," Leah told the supervisors, "this developer has promised you more revenue and better shopping and all kinds of goodies if you'll just give in.

"It's a devil's bargain. Here in Woodson, we don't treat our fellow citizens this way. We don't destroy the value of their homes and the quiet of their streets and the bonds of their community for shopping convenience.

"What if these were your homes? Would you want this done to them? What if these were your children playing in those streets and yards? Would you want the traffic tripled?

"There are places for these centers that don't threaten people. Where you don't have to seek this so-called 'variance' to put a massive center in. We know what we have here in Woodson. And we won't be overrun!"

The supervisors turned down the developer's request. Leah's reputation spread.

///

They were now able to pay the rent and utilities. To buy some new carpets. There was no fear of defaulting on the loan.

There was also plenty for Jill and Juan to do. So much, in fact, that Jerry and Leah now talked of hiring a new associate.

Jerry was in favor; Leah opposed. "I'm always fearful of a downturn," she said, "and I don't wish to lay anyone off." They would keep it under advisement.

Leah was especially fond of Jill, who reminded her of a younger version of herself. Jill seemed to her both tough and feminine, a good combination for any woman wanting to practice law.

Which was why Leah was surprised to catch her so somber in her office late one afternoon.

"What's the matter, dear?"

"Bob and I aren't getting along. We seem to be arguing every other night. Over nothing. We're just picking at every little fault. So different from the early months of marriage when we each could do no wrong."

"Has he hurt you? I mean physical violence."

"Oh no. Absolutely not. Just a constant squabble over this and that— who takes out the garbage; who goes to the cleaners and the grocery; who takes the car to the shop; whose night to cook and whose to do dishes. It's never-ending."

"I don't mean to make light of it, Jill, but it doesn't seem to me like the stuff that ends a marriage. Not yet anyway."

"Well, Mrs. Richards, what would you do?"

"I honestly can't advise you. I haven't been so perfect at marriage myself. But what you might do is lighten things up by making it a game."

"What do you mean?"

"For instance, by assigning points to chores. Two points for emptying the trash, seven for cutting the lawn, five for paying the monthly bills, two for changing a ceiling light bulb. You get the point."

"And the winner?"

"The winner, a three-month contest, gets to choose his or her favorite weekend destination for the two of you."

"Gosh," Jill said, "sounds kind of dull, reducing romance to arithmetic."

"Not at all. You'll be surprised what secret treasures you find in dailiness if you only look."

"Bob's gonna find the whole thing childish."

"Tell him people fall in love, or back in love, in childish ways. See Bob as half-full, not half-empty. He seems like a nice guy to me. Remember, too, there are no perfect men out there."

"Thanks, Mrs. Richards. He is a nice guy. At least, I look around at all these husbands, and I don't think I'd make a trade."

How odd, Leah thought, that she should ever be advising on this subject. But maybe not. You live and learn. I suppose everyone wonders at times, she said to herself, whether they should take their own advice.

///

TGIF is the great symbol of American workplace relief. For the young, it means happy hour. For Leah and Jerry, it meant time to kick back. Jerry had long legs; when he relaxed, he was a sprawler. Reclining had a nice feel. It had been a good but hectic week. They had earned every deep breath.

"I'd love nothing better than a four-day workweek," Jerry said. "A weekend is too short for errands. Monday comes before you know it."

"In your dreams, Jerry," Leah laughed. "We'd both be working five days or more, no matter what."

"You're right, Leah. Some people are just made that way. But even a workaholic is entitled to a dream."

"As well as some fun. Fly fishing this weekend?" Leah asked.

"Sure. Helen's given the green light."

"Why do you like it?"

"For the same reason trout like the stream; it's remote."

"But you throw them all back."

"Sure do. Can't visit capital punishment on a fish."

Suddenly, Jill swept into the room.

"Sorry for not knocking, Mrs. Richards, but there's a very agitated man demanding to see you. Thinks he's about to be arrested, wants you to defend him because he's heard you're the best."

Leah was alarmed when she stepped into the conference room but tried not to seem so.

The man appeared half-crazed, high on something, his eyes glazed and distant.

"Mr. Jones, that's the name, isn't it? You seem like a good man, but you need to calm down if we are to have a conversation."

Jerry, sensing trouble, brought the visitor a soft drink and sat down with the two of them.

"I'm being framed. My wife, the great love of my life, my everything, the mother to our kids, has been shot dead, and of course, they always think the husband did it. The police are questioning all the neighbors, trying to pin me, and I'm innocent!"

"Who did this?" Leah asked.

"I have no idea. Marsha never had an enemy."

"We can't solve all this now," said Leah, "and in the state you're in, don't talk to anyone. Not a single soul. You don't know what you'll come out with. Leave us your number. Ask the magistrate to appoint you a lawyer. Then tell her your story and let her tell that to the authorities."

Mr. Jones broke down weeping. "I'm innocent," he kept crying as he walked out the door. Those inside breathed a sigh of relief.

"Will you represent him?" Jerry said once he left.

"I'm over-committed on the criminal defense work, Jerry. I'm nervous I'll be spread too thin. Unfair to everyone."

"Do you believe him that he's innocent?"

"Not sure. He seemed so grieved about her as well as anxious about himself. The guilty ones are often wholly self-consumed. And the grief of his loss, you can understand, actually drew me to him."

"I think I believe him," interjected Jill, who had been listening outside the door.

"Maybe," Leah replied. "But that bulge in his coat pocket may just have been the murder weapon."

"We'll lock all the building entrances from now on," said Jerry. "Some TGIF."

///

The faculty at Woodson had discovered in Frank an aptitude for science. He was in eighth grade now, and John's friend, the high school chemistry teacher, had volunteered to help him with some weekend lab work.

"He's really quite the scientist," Louise told his parents.

"I don't understand where he gets it," Leah had said. "John and I are verbal people."

"I don't have to 'get' everything from you and dad," Frank protested. "Maybe my great-great-grandfather was some mad scientist, and it all just tunneled underground, until presto, it popped up in me."

"That's quite a theory, Frank," his father said. "Your mom and I have no better explanation."

He was growing up too fast for Leah. She knew she was not supposed to get weepy until he left for college, but this mother and son had been through so much together that she could not envision life without him.

True, they were arguing more now. Frank was thinking of himself incessantly, Leah thought, and he adamantly refused to smile for any pictures. To top it all off, he was bringing a classmate, Mary, by the house many afternoons, and it was obvious, as Leah watched his pieces move around the chessboard, that they liked each other a lot.

"Mom, Mary's really good at chess," Frank said when she left.

"Anything else?"

"C'mon, Mom. Watch the way she moves her knights and bishops."

"This has nothing to do with knights and bishops, Frank. I wasn't born yesterday."

"Don't you think it's a little early for all this?" Leah had called John in a state of mild alarm.

"Never too early, sweetheart. Or too late."

///

Frank suffered more than the usual teenage confusion. The relationship of his parents was incomprehensible. If two always-angry parents divorced, well he got that. But not this. His dad was his lifelong buddy. And he began to sense even through the spats with his mother that she was what his father had always known—a woman whose honesty, smarts, and decency inspired trust in those around her. So why were they not together? It didn't take a genius to see how much they were in love. Word of the affair had drifted his way, but it was a long, long ago abstract thing to him, and the revelation of it still left his parents inexplicable. Did their separation in some way have to do with him? Did they not want to be a family, whole and together? Or was it something more sinister and outlandish: Was he the product of an affair that no one would reveal?

"No, of course not," they both assured him. "You're what brings us together."

"Then why," he kept repeating. "Why?"

Apart from their separateness, they were, each in their own way, the best parents possible. He wanted no others. But why did he have no brothers or sisters? In spare moments, he used to imagine names and games with siblings that never were. Weren't parents like his made for children? Was he to spend his own life on questions no one would answer?

And well away, beyond the transmission of his thought, it was dawning on Leah that her life divided was not what she wished for her son.

CHAPTER

30

They were off to New Hampshire now to visit Frank at summer camp. Leah and John, Jenny and Deandra piled into John's old Ford which, as luck would have it, pulled off a rustic road with a flat.

"Sit right where you are," Deandra called as John was about to exit the car. "Leave it to me."

"Deandra, really, I can't let you do this."

"Why, John, because I'm female?" They rolled their eyes at each other. "Come off it. Are the spare, the jack, the lug wrench, and whatnot in the back?"

In just over twenty minutes, the tire was changed.

Deandra, back in the car, could see John was still nervous. "Okay, John, we'll stop at the next gas station and have someone check it out."

"Mighty fine job you did with that tire, mister," said the proprietor.

"Well, no, actually it was her," John responded.

"Really? Now my eyes have seen it all. See from the plates you folks are Pennsylvanians. Not to worry. It'll hold you a while."

"Deandra, where did you learn all this stuff?" John asked when they were back on the road.

"When I was a little girl riding with my parents, we had a flat. Didn't have a spare or anything. And we were thirsty. The road was lonely, but there were some passing cars, and several seemed to slow down to help until the drivers looked out and saw that we were black. What threat a ten-year-old child could possibly pose to them I'll never know. But from that moment on, I vowed to be independent in all things. And I kept that vow until I met Jenny. And now, mysteriously, I'm very dependent again, but in the most delicious way."

John, when he heard that, could not pass up the chance to squeeze Leah's hand.

It was Parents' Day at Camp Northern Trails, so named because its trails led deep into the surrounding woods and far up to Mount Washington and the other glorious peaks of the Presidential Range.

The camp was also on the shore of Newfound Lake, the third-largest of New Hampshire's famous inland lakes, as clear and beautiful as they were cold.

The little party stopped at Hebron for lunch and proceeded to meet an excited Frank, who was spending a happy summer on the archery and rifle ranges and learning how to canoe and sail.

"See, Dad, I got my Sharpshooter," Frank shouted as he ran up and brought out an artfully engraved riflery medal to show his father.

"I'm impressed," Deandra exclaimed as the party headed toward the waterfront for the sports that were to be the highlight of the day.

The festival did not disappoint. The tableau of brightly colored sails on the water thrilled even the landlubbers in the crowd, and the red and blue bandanaed oarsmen were now ready for the championship crew race.

"One-and-away, two-and-away," the coxswains' voices echoed across the lake, urging their charges into a sprint. And the oars feathered and gleamed in unison in the sunlight as sleek hulls glided through the clear water until red crew won by an exhausted hair.

"Yay," Frank yelled as he waved his own red bandana wildly.

Finally, the competition for best swimmer sent the seven freestyle finalists off and swimming toward a distant pole. They rounded the pole and were headed back to an unbearably excited crowd when Frank noticed his friend Peter was in trouble.

"Peter's cramping up," screamed Frank, but the rowboat, along to watch the swimmers, seemed not to notice.

This time, John did not hesitate. He dove in, swam in record time to the badly cramping, struggling boy. He swam down, down into the cold water to grab Peter and haul him the length of a football field and more to shore.

"Oh my God," wept his hysterical parents, hugging their young boy to whom first aid had now been administered. It was clear he was shaken but okay and he even managed a smile for his mom.

"That man saved me," he said, pointing to John.

"Yes, we know," his mother said, embracing John as only a relieved mother could.

The rest of the camp treated John as a hero. To Frank, whose father had always been heroic, he became even more so.

For Leah and John, the moment was more personal, touching the memory of a raft trip long ago.

"I hope that burden is lifted from you now," she said when she had some time alone with him. "It never, ever should have been yours to begin with."

"I'm just glad the boy was saved," was all he ever said.

///

Leah and John had enjoyed the drive back from New Hampshire with Jenny and Deandra. Each young woman had completed her education, and both were testing the job market.

"Have you thought of a regional hospital near Woodson?" Leah asked Jenny. "And Deandra, maybe you could team with friends on a dinner theater in town. It would be a cultural boost for our community. Think of the Barter Theater and all it's meant for Abingdon."

"Thanks," said Jenny, "and we'd love to be near you. But we're urban creatures. We love the city, and it's not clear how much mixed-race lesbian couples would be welcomed in Woodson. That's the hell of it. The map of this country is so splotchy. Especially a politically polka-dotted swing state like Pennsylvania. Safe little enclaves in parts of Philadelphia, Pittsburgh, Harrisburg, and then miles upon miles of rural countryside where we'd have to always be on guard. Not to overly stereotype."

"I get what you mean. Some people have a harder time embracing differences than others. But this is an issue where it's tough to see the intolerant side," replied Leah.

"Yeah," added Deandra. "We're just going about our lives, not judging or bugging anybody. And what we're asking is so simple. Please, won't you just leave us alone?"

"That's the thing though, no one really exists alone. Look at Woodson. Small town, everyone knows everyone else's business. You depend on the local grocer for your food, the local pharmacist for your medication, even the local attorney for your legal issues. There's no way to exist without interacting with others. So, it's good to know what they think. Maybe at least some well-meaning traditionalists have a point in valuing what they value," ventured Leah. "Even if your outlook of simply accepting everyone is much better. Their point is that men and women still serve very different family roles for so many people."

"All very rational and cool with me if that's how they want to live," Deandra replied. "But Jen and I want a family too. We'll make great parents—that I promise you. So, no, I don't concede for a minute that so-called nice traditionalists have a point in having an opinion on our lives. Because they don't get the privilege of making a point if they haven't lived through the bigotry."

If you haven't lived through it, Leah thought to herself, remembering her talks with Nancy.

The whole thing caused Leah to reflect on her home community. "Most of the people of Woodson would be welcoming to you both, I think. But," she conceded, "there's some who would take offense. Old die-hards. And it takes only a few mean ones to cause trouble. Anyway, Deandra, I was just dreaming that your dinner theater might help lure John back to town."

John kept on driving. But it was clear he appreciated the sentiment.

Things were now much quieter. Each traveler was exhausted by the near tragedy at the lake and the long hours in the car.

Glancing in the mirror at the couple in the back—who had their heads resting on one another—Leah finally broke the silence. "I'm so glad you two are together," she said. "You're a wonderful fit. I keep thinking how happy Hank would be to see you now."

CHAPTER

31

The firm of Richards and Yates had reached a crossroads. It had been successful. Leah and Jerry now had all the business they needed and then some. Clients were starting to come from outside town. They had hired that third associate and were thinking of a fourth and fifth, but this time it was Jerry who called a pause.

"Do we really want to go big, Leah?" he asked. "Just because clients show up at the door doesn't mean we have to take them in."

Leah was torn. "Doesn't it seem almost a sacrilege to turn down business? When we first started, we'd have given our eyeteeth for any one of these chances."

"All true, but remember what we left Philadelphia to escape. I want my time with Helen, Tim, and my little daughter. And I love my fly-fishing, just a few moments between the stream and myself."

"I get that, but if we make a real go of it, don't we open up things for our children too?"

They didn't have to decide it immediately. Leah needed to talk it over with John.

"I think I should do this for Frank," she said to John later that evening. "There's college and grad school on the horizon."

"You're making a good bit as is," he replied.

"Okay, but I just want to be a conventional success at something. Maybe it's selfish of me, but I want to go to my Harvard reunions and have my classmates recognize who I am."

"Isn't it more important that you recognize yourself?"

"That's the problem, John. I never really have."

After much thought, Leah acceded. She and Jerry had worked well together. They needed to be on the same page as to the future of the firm.

And Frank was now a teenager. Whether he knew it or not, he would need her.

"All right, Jerry. Ouch, we'll turn down business at the door. But one of these days, maybe when the kids leave for college and we both need the money, you'll be the one stepping into my office with, 'Leah, we've got to go big.'"

Unbeknownst to Jerry and John, Leah's old friend Bill had called recently, asking her to serve on the planning committee for their twentieth class reunion. Bill's career had taken off. He was serving as general counsel for Morgan Stanley and earning more in salary, bonuses, and stock options than Leah back in Woodson could ever hope for. Hearing Bill's voice had brought back their time at Harvard. Now, as then, Leah could not stop imagining other roads in the wood or resist the need to make comparisons.

///

On the weekends John came into town, he and Leah would occasionally resume their old front-porch habit of bird watching.

"Leah, do you know what I like about cardinals?"

"No, what?"

"That it's so easy to tell the guys from the dolls."

"Foolish, silly boy," Leah laughed as she tickled his ribs. "What am I to do with you?"

"Just what you used to," he said hopefully.

He was indeed her court jester. Not just hers, because she could imagine him in the halls of Tudor kings adding levity to their banquets of venison and wine. And her jester also had his serious and literary sides, which she was not at all sure his jester ancestors possessed. It was this ability of his, this way of tapping the range of her, that made her want him, badly, even as the mellowness of the early fall evening induced in John his most reflective state of mind.

"Well, I never thought I'd say it, but we're getting older."

"I don't know, John. I'm willing to bet we are still spry."

Perhaps her hint was too subtle, as it quite passed him by.

"You know, Leah, Thoreau knew the secret to life was to know one place really well. Woodson's no Walden Pond, but each of us has spent a good chunk of our lives here, and I'd say we know its rhythms well."

"It's not just knowing the rhythms of one place, John, but the rhythms of one person."

This time, apparently, the hint was not subtle. They hurried off the porch together and flicked off the outdoor lights in record time.

Leah found herself driving to Allentown on a midweek mission. Frank would stay with his friend and classmate Tim at Jerry's house while she went to see John. She felt her stomach churning because this visit was not an ordinary one.

He had been expecting her. He suspected something she didn't want to discuss on the phone.

Leah rehearsed at length what she might say before she decided to charge right in. "John, it's not my habit, as you know, to dance around. It's time you come home."

He was not entirely surprised. "I can't just leave the school system here in Allentown in the lurch."

"I'm not suggesting you do. But the school year ends three months from now, and William will make the move go smoothly."

"But where would I work? I can't go back to Woodson High. Frank will be there, and there's too much history."

"I've already talked to Winslow." Leah had used her professional connections to secure a phone call with the head of the private school right outside the town of Woodson. "It just so happens they have an opening, and they love your résumé."

"Opening at the high school?"

"Yes."

"My, you've thought of everything."

"One thing you and I both need to think of. Frank's a teenager now. There's many a speeding ticket and underage beer can in his future. And we're lucky if that's all there is. He needs a full-time father. Think how happy this would make him."

"Well, Leah, you're right he needs us both, so what you're saying makes good sense."

"So you'll come?"

"Is it only for Frank's sake, or do you want me?"

She was overjoyed at his reaction. "You know the answer to that as well as I do."

///

The news of John's return spread rapidly. Already, Leah and Nancy were planning a homecoming party.

"We have to make it a two-house party," Nancy insisted. "There's way too many folks to fit in yours."

Every kind of foodstuff was prepared. Every bush strung with lights. John's favorite fiddler and guitarist were engaged.

"But what if," worried Leah.

"What if what?"

"What if it rains."

"It wouldn't dare," exclaimed Nancy. "John's coming home!"

The guest list exploded. Jerry and his family. Jill and Bob. Juan and his family. William and his. The Hinkles and several of Leah's old friends from the firm. John's friends Henry and Louise and others he liked especially at Woodson High. Jenny and Deandra from Philadelphia. Some of Frank's friends and their families from school. People whom they had long known in the neighborhood. Giovanni, who had retired, and his son who now ran the restaurant. Once again, Katie made the cut. Ellen, to whom Leah gave no more than a fleeting thought, did not.

It was, Leah thought, like a curtain call at the end of a favorite play. The entire cast assembled, the audience applauding. They were blessed to have such friends.

33

The party never came about. John called Leah the week of the party with some sad news that couldn't wait till he saw her in person. He had not been feeling at all well. For weeks he had been losing weight and experiencing abdominal pain. He was accustomed to shaking off such things, as he thought guys should do, but it was suddenly too much. He had gone to the doctor and received the diagnosis just that afternoon.

Pancreatic cancer. "The big P," he joked grimly. Stage IV. It had reached the liver. Maybe one month to live.

"It's an odd thing. You feel all your life you're impregnable. Until one day you aren't.

"Will you tell Frank tonight? You'll know just how to put it. I'll speak with him tomorrow. And could you have Nancy tell the rest?"

"John, when can I see you?"

"I'll be at home here in Allentown. As long as I can stand it. Then I'll go to the medical center here. They're good doctors, kind people, and they know my case."

She went to Allentown immediately. The disease was on the march, and already she found him hospitalized.

She waited and inquired and waited some more. Nurses and doctors brushed by; unknown figures on unknowable missions. Each second seemed sadder than the second before.

When she feared the end was near, she sent for Frank. William brought him up. It was all so sudden. Reality had not broken through to them.

///

When Leah and Frank arrived one morning at the family waiting room, she was stunned to find Ellen and her husband.

Stunned and angry.

What was Ellen doing here at a time like this? At the funeral perhaps her presence could be excused. Or the wake. But not here, at the saddest and most intimate of hours.

Leah stared at the two of them. Ellen was trying to claim a status that was not hers. She was trying to pretend nothing had happened, that she had done nothing wrong.

Leah hardly knew Ellen's husband but thought he must be weak, letting her come.

Frank saw his mother was distraught and tried to calm her. "She's just trying to be nice, Mom," he said.

For John's sake, she would not make a scene.

///

Leah found herself that afternoon driving the short distance from the hospital back to John's. He had wanted to die with one of his books by his side.

Her mind was a tangle of dark thoughts. Why was John dying in Allentown? Why not Woodson? Or even Philadelphia? Allentown, Pennsylvania. It might as well have been Allentown, France. Death, she decided, when it comes, should not come in strange places.

Her anger returned upon recalling Ellen. John and Frank no doubt saw her presence as a gesture of kindness. Leah was much less sure. Was Ellen trying to express some lingering love of her own for John, some regret for a life of theirs that might have been? It seemed almost diabolical. Was it not enough that Ellen did what she did? Would her sister never leave her in peace?

At the house, she took her time with John's books. So many titles so familiar to her, even if their precise placement on the shelves was not. She recalled their discussions, their little always-in-session book club of two. It would make her miss him even more. At last, she found it. The book he wanted was *Jane Eyre*. Leah thought she knew why. After years of separation, a reunion in the end.

///

She came back to his bedside. Stared in disbelief at a Get Well Soon card. She tried not to seem sad. Her poor husband was so diminished, an intravenous mess.

He was glad to see her. She sat down at the bedside and held his hand.

Swallowing was hard. Speaking harder. Far beyond his capacity was the pleasure of a yawn or a deep breath.

Finally, "Will you forgive me?" he said.

She squeezed his hand. "John, I love you so. I always will."

"Will you forgive me?"

She was quiet. She worked her way around the tubing and pressed her cheek against his. She did love him, only him, but she could not forget the thing that set in motion such sad consequences for them all.

She was exhausted. More so than ever in her life. She would try to catch a few hours' sleep and come back first thing the next morning. She would bring some cut tulips to brighten things up.

That night, John passed away with Frank at his side.

34

Many months passed. Frank had something he wanted to know. In one of their last talks, his dad had passed these words to him: "Tell your mom to love the squirrels."

"I can't understand what Dad was getting at."

Leah laughed. She had almost forgotten how. She remembered all too well John's elegies to squirrels. Their soft white underbellies, the white fringe on their bushy tails, their bodies agile on a tree trunk—John tried to make their case. "Pests, John, pests," she had insisted.

"Mom, I keep wondering what Dad meant."

"Frank, your father was quite the tease. But he loved all living creatures."

"Even squirrels?"

"Even them."

"How come?"

"Here, Frank. This book is from Dad. One of his favorites. It's by James Herriot: *All Creatures Great and Small*."

///

John's death made Leah think back every now and then to high school and the strange directions life took, even when she wasn't aware of them. As Leah's life had headed east, an old high-school classmate traveled west. Gloria had received a promotion to assistant manager of a new Comfort Lodge near Pittsburgh. Leaving Woodson had not been a hard decision.

The promotion was a big step up, her parents had passed on, and she had no friends, at least none to speak of, that she'd be leaving behind.

Gloria knew she was not a perfect person. But she had begun to rationalize and reimagine things as well. Such unhappiness as had befallen her was not all her fault. Hunters shot and killed deer during the season, and what had the deer done? What had she done other than, like the deer, try to stay out of harm's way? And if people were going to take aim at her, she, unlike the deer, had the means of fighting back.

"Welcome to Pittsburgh, Ms. Jackson," said her new manager.

"It's good to be here."

"People still think of Pittsburgh as a steel town. That's almost insulting, it's so out of date. Anyway, you can think of us as a sports town, if you will. The Pirates, Steelers, Penguins—black and yellow are our colors; you can tell a Pittsburgh team from miles away. Here's a Pirates cap for you. Quite a distinctive P. A good conversation starter."

"I'm afraid sports aren't really my thing. I never much went to games at Woodson High."

"That could change in a hurry. People refer to us as a small market which, of course, only builds up the spirit. Our teams don't just play on the field. You can almost feel their presence in bars and grills, over beer and pretzels."

The conversation only left Gloria feeling disconnected. She returned to her apartment wondering how she would ever build rapport with this rah-rah, and to make matters worse, her TV was on the fritz. She thought impulsively of returning to Woodson, but going back in time was impossible when every bridge from the past had been burnt.

Her apartment, especially in the early dark of winter, had come to seem cold. Her cozy chairs of childhood now returned her gaze with silence. She realized she was growing old alone, staring at a past for which there seemed no replay or retraction. She had kept in her wallet a snapshot of herself as a young beauty, but the picture with the passing years brought mainly moments of reckoning, so she put it in a drawer where it would seldom be seen. Age brought, in time, a softening instinct to say

"I'm sorry," but that idea departed almost before it arrived because she didn't know to whom she could ever manage to say it.

Still, she thought back on occasion to her Woodson days. The wreckage of the Richards family had at first brought her such a sense of accomplishment, but, as time went on, a twinge of genuine regret. She had heard of John's death and even thought of writing Leah but supposed it would bring more anguish than comfort. There was no mortal left to forgive her, only a chance to forgive herself, and that meant starting anew almost incognito. Therein lay hope. Perhaps people in Woodson would one day forget there had ever been such a person as Gloria Jackson, and people in Pittsburgh would come to say, "Don't let that sad face deceive you, she's really not so bad."

///

Some years passed. "Mom, why don't you call Aunt Ellen?" Frank asked one day out of the blue. Startled at the question, Leah pled ignorance of Ellen's cell number.

Frank had started medical school at Penn, and Leah came up to visit often.

"Mom, Aunt Ellen's still family." Frank thought of the affair as deeply hurtful but also as something very long ago.

"Frank, you are my family," Leah said, taking his hand.

"It's just strange, the two of you down there in Woodson, never speaking."

"You know the law practice is just about all that I can handle."

"I keep thinking Dad would want you to do this. Isn't that how we keep someone's memory fresh, by doing things for them, as if they were still here?"

"Sometimes, son, it's best to let the past stay past. The less I think about that, the more I am at peace."

"I'm not sure I believe that, Mom," he said, hugging her. Their conversation drifted to more comfortable terrain.

It was the first time Frank had become instructional with her, Leah thought as she headed back to Woodson. In a sense, children end up becoming parents, she supposed.

Philadelphia to Woodson. Woodson to Philadelphia. She had memorized the road, every bend, exit, rise, and fall of it. She even knew the spots on the Schuylkill Expressway where she would likely have to hit the brakes. The most familiar roads still carry complete strangers, she thought, as she wondered what problems all those other drivers had. Whether their problems were perpetual, whether all lives were riddles never wholly solved.

///

When Leah came back from work each evening, the first thing she did was check the mail. The usual dreary assortment of utility bills, solicitations, bank statements, coupons and catalogs, pre-sorted standard stuff, enlivened only by a special offering to Harvard graduates to cruise down the Rhine, which she supposed few would ever find the time to take. All rather sad, she thought, as she remembered how her family once eagerly awaited deliveries from the post office of yore.

Suddenly her eye caught a handwritten letter in the pile with 'Jackson' as the name on the return address. Jackson? Did she know a Jackson?

> *Dear Leah,*
>
> *It has taken me a long time to find the courage to write this letter, which I hope finds you well. It is so sad about John's passing; he loved you so.*
>
> *I should not ask you to forgive me for the way I treated your family because I could never forgive myself. But if you could find it in your heart to forgive me anyway, it would mean a lot.*
>
> *I am not who I once was. I am in the hospitality business these days, Comfort Lodge to be exact. If your travels ever bring you to Pittsburgh, you might let me know and your accommodations will be the best.*
>
> *I hope Ellen is doing well. I've lost touch with her, and indeed with most of my Woodson schoolmates. Please do give her my very best.*
>
> *I wish you only the best.*
>
> *Sincerely,*
> *—Gloria*

Leah's first impulse was to tear the letter up; her second to set it aside. The past once again seemed perversely determined never to let go. Ultimately, she decided she would return to the letter one of these days when her spirit allowed.

She told herself from time to time that she really did intend to respond. But things kept coming up, and she never did.

Many years passed. Leah found herself aging into the bittersweet of life.

She had moved back to Philadelphia to be near Frank. He had remained her pride and joy, a pediatric nephrologist, happily married with two special daughters in high school, where their grandmother could be part of their lives.

Frank and William had stayed friends and went together to some Flyers games. "Your parents," William said to Frank during a break in the action. "I've known 'em together and I've known 'em apart. Two of the finest people who ever lived."

Jenny and Deandra came to visit Leah regularly, with Hank, their adopted son.

But mostly her friends had passed along. Mr. Hinkle and Jim and Nancy Ferguson had died some years back, taking much of the best of old Woodson with them.

Jerry had succumbed to cancer. A man Leah never thought she'd miss, she sorely did. Still, Tim was instructing Frank in Jerry's old love of fly fishing with, as Tim gently put it, "mixed success."

Gloria never once returned to Woodson. Few seemed to care. Her wish not to be remembered badly had been granted, in the sense that she was scarcely remembered at all.

Peace had settled on Leah's life. Or had it? Some circles never close. Some ends are never tied.

"I think I was too hard on John," Leah mused one day to Katie.

Katie had softened, but not much.

"Nonsense, dear. That man destroyed your family. Let your brother drown. Defiled your sister. Save your guilt."

Katie was so off-base. She left Leah more alone. It was all on her now.

Leah returned home one evening after a nice dinner with her granddaughters. She had glimpsed but never wholly grasped just how much of an inspiration she had been in their lives. She lifted her eyes as if to find inspiration above the trees and rooftops, far, far up. The last pink tincture was departing the sky, taking with it the reminder that there was ever such a thing as day.

Home, as always, was her comfort. She looked once more at her small table and the picture of John.

She never did seek that divorce. They were separated but remained husband and wife, parents, and friends until the day he died. Had life allowed it, they might have aged together. Shared their past, their grandchildren, and faced infirmities with one another. All their old love, at different stages, might have been theirs again.

Her pain still flickered. Once upon a time, the pain of his adultery. Now, the pain of feeling she let pass all that might have been.

Acceptance. He was one of the kindest human beings ever to walk the earth, but so often she desired him to be "successful," something more. She had never stopped loving him. Not since she was a child. Not since he was her playmate in the old front yard. The one she loved most had hurt her most, but it was she who had been given, over and over in her lifetime, the chance to forgive.

She sank back in her chair. The recognition, held at bay for many years, now hit her hard.

It was she who must ask him to forgive.

"John, will you forgive me?" she spoke aloud.

The silence descended once more.

"John, will you forgive me?" her voice quaked.

A deeper silence now. A long quest begun.

In whatever dim corner of the universe she might find him, she thought he would say yes.

///

The next week, Leah picked up the phone.

"Ellen?"

"Leah." Ellen's voice was soft with remembrance.

It was but a start. But a start far better than the silences of so many years before.

ACKNOWLEDGMENTS

My aunt Lucille Penniman unknowingly initiated this novel when, on my visits to her in West Chester, she regaled me about Pennsylvania and its many splendors. Her son Charles, a devotee of the Franklin Institute, worked as a minister in Philadelphia. Both Pennimans have passed on but left me with an abiding fascination with the Keystone State in all of its diversity and variety. So much variety, in fact, that my heroine, Leah, cannot fully decide where in Pennsylvania she wants to live. I hope my fellow Virginians will forgive my affection for two states with such rich histories and that my fellow lawyers will pardon my dream of writing a romance novel. 'Virginia is for Lovers' our welcome signs proclaim, but surely, love with all its heartache and glory, can break out in another commonwealth.

I am indebted to several readers whom I can always count on for candor: Ed Barber, Karen Henderson, Barbara Perry, and Sophia Veltfort. Their suggestions werc invaluable. A special note of thanks to Louis Capozzi, a distinguished Pennsylvanian who never tires of singing the praises of his native state.

It has been such a pleasure to work with the fine team at Sunbury Press. Thanks to Lawrence Knorr, Marianne Babcock, Fen Alankus, Chris Fenwick, and Joe Walters for their cheerful encouragement and support. To cover designer Ashley Shumaker and book designer Crystal Devine: I owe the aesthetics of the final product to your fine skills.

My deep gratitude goes to my editor, Jennifer Cappello. Jennifer has made one terrific suggestion after another. She brings to her craft an intuitive sense of the book. All authors should be so lucky.

ABOUT THE AUTHOR

J. HARVIE WILKINSON III is a federal judge whose life was touched by so many romantic novels that he set out to write one himself. He is a Circuit Judge on the United States Court of Appeals for the Fourth Circuit. He has served as a law clerk to Justice Lewis Powell of the United States Supreme Court, as a professor at the University of Virginia Law School, Editorial Page Editor of a large metropolitan newspaper (the *Norfolk Virginian-Pilot*), and Deputy Assistant Attorney General in the Civil Rights Division of the Department of Justice.

Judge Wilkinson was awarded the Thomas Jefferson Medal by the University of Virginia and the Thomas Jefferson Foundation, the highest outside award offered by the university. He was awarded the Lawrenceville Medal, the highest award given by the Lawrenceville School. He is a Fellow of the American Academy of Arts and Sciences.

He is also the author of several books: *Harry Byrd and the Changing Face of Virginia Politics*, 1968; *Serving Justice: A Supreme Court Clerk's View*, 1974; *From Brown to Bakke: The Supreme Court and School Integration*, 1979; *One Nation Indivisible: How Ethnic Separatism Threatens America*, 1997; *Cosmic Constitutional Theory: Why Americans Are Losing Their Inalienable Right to Self-Governance*, 2012; and *All Falling Faiths: Reflections on the Promise and Failure of the 1960s*, 2017.

Judge Wilkinson lives in Charlottesville, Virginia. He and his wife, Lossie, have two children, Nelson and Porter, and three grandchildren.